PENGUIN BOOKS

T0358008

Growing up in rural New Zealand, Amanda Hampson was determined to be a writer from an early age. She moved to London in her twenties where she fell in love with British literature and developed a fascination for the complexities of British culture.

Eventually settling in Australia, she has a particular interest in the themes of place, family and the meaning of home. She now lives in Sydney's Northern Beaches.

The Olive Sisters was her highly successful debut novel, followed by *Two for the Road*. She has also written two non-fiction books.

The FRENCH Perfumer

AMANDA HAMPSON

PENGUIN BOOKS

PENGUIN BOOKS

UK | USA | Canada | Ireland | Australia
India | New Zealand | South Africa | China

Penguin Books is part of the Penguin Random House group of companies
whose addresses can be found at global.penguinrandomhouse.com.

First published by Penguin Random House Australia Pty Ltd, 2017
This edition published by Penguin Random House Australia Pty Ltd, 2018

1 3 5 7 9 10 8 6 4 2

Cover design by Nikki Townsend Design © Penguin Random House Australia Pty Ltd
Text design by Samantha Jayaweera © Penguin Random House Australia Pty Ltd
Illustrations by Kymba © Penguin Random House Australia Pty Ltd
Cover photographs: main image, Tracy Packer Photography/Getty Images; magnolia,
Neslihan Rawles/Getty Images; background, Slobo/Getty Images
Typeset in Garamond by Samantha Jayaweera, Penguin Random House Australia Pty Ltd
Printed and bound in Australia by Griffin Press, an accredited ISO AS/NZS 14001
Environmental Management Systems printer.

National Library of Australia
Cataloguing-in-Publication data:

Hampson, Amanda, author.
The french perfumer / Amanda Hampson.
9780143788508 (paperback)
Subjects: Perfumes--Fiction.
France--Fiction.

penguin.com.au

For Catherine, with love

Chapter One

My first day in France! I surely must have known that the French drive on the wrong side of the road; nevertheless it took me completely by surprise. It is only by sheer good luck that I have even survived my first day. Paris may be romantic arm-in-arm with your lover but for a woman alone and disorientated, it is nothing short of terrifying. My schoolgirl French turns out to be hopeless. I might as well be surrounded by people speaking in chemical formulae or algebra equations.

Throughout the miserable grey drizzle of the channel crossing to Calais, I was dizzy with nerves and a sort of horrified fascination at my daring. By the time I stepped off the train at Gare du Nord in Paris, my anxiety had billowed into blind terror. I had been given directions to a hotel booked on my behalf, not far from the station, and spent a good part of the journey poring over the map obsessively.

Exiting the station, I was ambushed by a beggar thrusting her filthy hand at me and gabbling wildly. I would have happily given her something as I have been furnished with some French francs for incidentals (although it was impressed upon me that every centime must be accounted for) but daren't reach for my purse lest she snatch it. So, ditching all dignity, I sidestepped and scuttled off with my suitcase clasped to my chest. What a blessing that the map was seared into my mind – proof that anxiety can sometimes be good preparation.

Now, ensconced in a tiny hotel room, Paris life seethes all around me but I'm too nervous to leave my room. Whatever made me think I could do something like this? Thankfully I packed some sandwiches and a thermos of tea to keep me going; that will be my supper tonight.

Paris is all behind me now. Leaving the hotel in the blur of dawn, the taxi thudding over cobblestones and careening down narrow streets, I was fearful I'd be lost deep in that city, never to be found. I made a feeble attempt with the driver but apparently my pronunciation of Gare de Lyon was not to his liking as he snarled, '*Garrrrderrrrleeoon!*' On reflection, I may actually have said *guerre* which I am almost certain means war, not railway station – my first diplomatic blunder.

I am now on the train travelling through flat, rural landscapes comfortingly reminiscent of the home counties. It is quite a journey down the length of France to Cannes but I have my book – Miss Christie's latest – should I get bored. I had hoped to refresh my thermos with tea at the hotel but that proved well beyond my language capability. Really, did we learn a single practical phrase in Mrs Barker's French class? You would expect being able to order tea would be the highest priority.

Initially it seemed I might have the first-class compartment to myself, which would have been ideal as I barely slept a wink last night. But as the train pulled out of the station, a handsome young man burst into the compartment and flung himself into the corner next to the window. He exuded the pleasant yeasty smell of decadence and was dressed in the style of the Romantic poets: emerald-green velvet jacket over a white voluminous shirt. No luggage. He pulled his hat down over his eyes and was asleep in trice.

An older gentleman then arrived in the compartment and spent an inordinate amount of time settling his bag into the luggage rack, removing his coat and hat and making himself comfortable on the bench opposite me. He has infused the tiny space with the acrid odour of French cigarettes undercut by a cloying *eau de cologne*. He offered some pleasantries and I apologised for being English, but now, despite my ignoring him as I write, he watches me with a suggestive smile as though he finds me mildly amusing. Behind that smile I sense a ruined man, one with that dark, rotten place concealed inside many men these days; those who endured the horror of not one but two wars. Suffering hollowed out their core, gouged away any tenderness. As it did my father, who had a fury simmering inside him that could reach boiling point in a split second.

Dear departed Father, difficult as he was, impossible as he could be, in the right frame of mind he could be witty and clever and excellent company. He read widely and voraciously and was deeply knowledgeable. In earlier days, and especially when it was just the two of us throughout the war, we had many pleasant evenings in front of the fire. His mood mellowed by alcohol, he talked to me about politics, history, literature, philosophy . . . We discussed a great many things over his last years. The only taboo subject was that of Mother. But enough about Father. If the only thing I achieve with this venture is to crawl out from under his shadow — that would be a marvellous thing in itself.

I have been instructed to wait in the lobby of the Carlton Hotel in Cannes where my new employer's driver will collect me. However, when I arrived this evening and saw how impossibly grand it is, I decided to park myself on my suitcase on the pavement outside. Then, realising I was conspicuous in my shabby tweed coat, I began to worry that I might be mistaken for a refugee from some impoverished Eastern European country. On top of that, there was a salty wind gusting off the bay, so I have now relocated to an armchair in the lobby and probably look quite important scribbling in my notebook.

My train journey did improve. The young man awoke an hour or so into the trip and asked me the time. I really have to stop being startled when spoken to in French. This is France. It's unavoidable. On discovering I was English, he was immediately curious and peppered me with questions. The unpleasant older man was so disturbed by our chatter that he made quite a show of departing for more peaceful climes.

The young man, Alexander, also from London, had gone to Paris for a party and was now on his way home to Cannes. I am not normally in the habit of conversing with strange men but there was something kindly about him — a depth beyond his years — and, despite his bohemian bravado, a curious vulnerability. He was terribly impressed at me resigning my position after seventeen years in the civil service for a short-term post in the South of France. The need for honesty led me to disclose that, far from being one of those intrepid, independent women who welcomes challenge and seeks adventure, my best strengths are procrastination and obstacle enumeration. His laughter is the bubbling, infectious variety that encouraged me to make further self-deprecating observations and feel rather witty.

We talked all the way to Cannes and, although he revealed little detail about himself, I found myself chatting with him as though we were already friends. He asked me what possessed me to make the rash decision to leave my job for this little jaunt and I explained it was because of Colleen and my dear little cat, Mitzi.

Colleen was my closest friend in the department. There are so many things I like about her, one being that she smells of generosity and kindness which is very comforting, like the aroma of warm scones or flannelette sheets. She has a wild Irish sense of humour and can even wring a laugh out of Mrs Mickelson, the cantankerous tea lady who inflicts her bitter tea and soft biscuits on our section twice a day.

On Fridays, Colleen and I always had lunch together, just the two of us. Rain, hail or shine, we'd walk briskly to the Lyons' Corner House on the Strand and secure our seats before the lunch rush set in. Colleen always teased me about having the same dish – grilled gammon – but it suited me because supper could just be bread and butter and a pot of tea. On the way, Colleen always bought the latest copy of *The Lady* (she is endeavouring to become more refined) and would read the Personals aloud to me, particularly the advertisements of gentlemen seeking secretaries or housekeepers with the object of matrimony 'if suited'. These secretaries and housekeepers are invariably required to be attractive, refined, discreet and sometimes to have 'means' as well. Younger women are preferred, regardless of the age of the gentleman. Occasionally there are specific preferences such as a particular weight or must like children, dogs or hunting, and the more jaded advertisers added the caveat, 'No triflers'.

Colleen would always urge me to enter into correspondence with any gentleman she thought suitable but truly my only qualification is that I am definitely not a trifler – more's the pity. I did sometimes wonder what my requirements might be. Certainly no expectations about appearance. So long as he was tender, kind and fairly interesting, I wouldn't mind a little stoutness or even jug ears. I would draw the line at knock-knees or a stoop, however. Good posture is important to me. Attentive, affectionate, but not overly so. I wouldn't care to be pawed. A sense of humour would count for a great deal too . . .

Where was I? Back to the day in question. Colleen's attention was drawn to a particular ad: 'Shorthand typist required by English speaker in the South of France. Live-in, full board plus salary commensurate with experience. Appointment for 3–4 months.' She looked up from the newspaper, her face radiant with excitement. 'Iris! That would be the making of you. South of France!' She ripped it out with a flourish and passed it to me.

'I don't see how I could possibly go away for so long,' I said.

She wasn't listening, but pointing out the details. 'You have to apply in writing to a solicitor in Belgravia. Come on, what do you say?'

'Are you trying to get rid of me?' I teased.

She clasped my hands in hers. 'Iris, you've been in the civil service for seventeen years! You've given your youth to it. You're thirty-five years old! Your life is half over. I cannot stand to see you mouldering away in that dreary mausoleum for the rest of your life without ever having done anything . . . anything impulsive or outrageous. Without ever having properly lived.'

'Colleen, I am living. I'm perfectly happy with my life.' (That part was not strictly true.) 'Besides, what would I do with Mitzi?'

'Oh,' she said scornfully, 'I didn't think of that. Of course, your devotion to your cat would certainly be a valid reason not to embark on any sort of adventure.' Devotion, she pointed out, is not a feline trait. Mitzi was as pragmatic as any other cat. 'She'd be perfectly happy with Mrs Whats-it next door. If you think about it, Iris, that's just an excuse. And a rather feeble one at that.'

There was not a whisker of a chance I would do something like this of my own accord but when Colleen realised she couldn't bully me into it, I caught a glimpse of the same disappointed resignation in her eyes that I had recently seen in my brother's. And I felt that same chill as though seeing myself quite dispassionately. I know that Alan has given up on me, but to lose the respect and affection of Colleen would be almost unendurable. And if that wasn't enough to propel me into action, a week later my dear little Mitzi died, taking my last excuse with her.

Mitzi was my friend and companion; she was family. One evening during the blitz when I couldn't face another night sleeping packed in like sardines in Balham Station, I hunkered down in the cupboard under the stairs with Mitzi. That very night a bomb dropped right into the station and killed all those poor people sheltering there. The only time I ever saw Father cry was when he returned from his Home Guard shift and found us alive. I felt vindicated that I did not have Mitzi destroyed at the start of the war when the government convinced people to put down tens of thousands of pets because they weren't allowed in the public air raid shelters. I took the chance. I saved her life and she saved mine. I wouldn't have chosen to stay in the house alone. So we were bonded, and I took her passing as a sign.

It wasn't just that. There was also an incident at work that gave me pause for thought.

One lunchtime a few of the girls in the department went off to the King's Head after work to celebrate Shirley's engagement. I was invited by default, simply because everyone was going. It's not that I'm disliked or unpopular, just often overlooked. Shirley is the opposite. Around the office she was considered quite the honey pot and it's hardly surprising she was engaged. When she first joined the department, like many of my colleagues I was in something of a thrall. We all wanted to be her friend and bask in her radiance. But it was not to be.

That afternoon at the pub, she had gone up to the bar to buy the first round and we girls – six of us – were settling ourselves in the snug. Irene offered to take coats. I was cold so kept mine on and shimmied around on the half-circle banquette so the others could sit either side of me when they had finished happily piling their coats on Irene. I was enjoying the warm, convivial atmosphere of laughter but because of the shenanigans with the coats I was alone on the banquette when Shirley came back with a tray of drinks. She saw me across the table and said, 'Oh, I'm terribly sorry . . .' She then half-turned toward the empty seating closer to the open fire.

I didn't know what to say. There was a long awkward moment before Colleen realised Shirley's error and whispered my name in her ear. To give Shirley credit, she was mortified and could not apologise enough. 'Iris! I'm so dreadfully sorry. I'm half blind without my specs, you know,' she laughed. 'With the light behind you . . .'

'I understand,' I said. 'Please don't worry.' The fuss simply drew more attention to a moment that could just as easily have slipped by unnoticed. It is one thing being overlooked, but quite another being made the centre of attention at the same time.

Colleen slipped in beside me, laughing. 'Dear ol' Iris – you're a chameleon. It's your gift. She thought you were part of the decor.' The girls all laughed. I broke out my smile and tried to join in. I realised in that moment that I was part of the decor in the department too. Like an outdated but useful piece of furniture, I was requisitioned to other departments and returned when not required. I still remembered a time when I hoped for much more. It was the final glimmer of that hope that made me take this chance. And here I was on my way to the French Riviera.

The atmosphere in the carriage was charged by Alexander's enthusiasm for my adventure and my spirits lifted as the landscape began to change for the better, more reminiscent of picture postcards of the French Riviera. The flat landscape gave way to undulating woodlands. To our right, the sea glittered in the sun. The trees were strange twisted pines and thin pointy ones, interspersed by cream stucco villas with red terracotta roofs. To our left, the landscape was all cliffs and rocky escarpments.

I told Alexander about my interview for the position with my employer's solicitor, Mr Hubert. On offering me the position, he had made a slightly worrying comment that it was 'a bit of an odd situation' and therefore better suited to someone of my maturity. The phrase captured Alexander's imagination and he spent the last part of the journey speculating on all kinds of outlandish scenarios. These seemed amusing at the time but less so now that I am here dwelling on them while waiting for the driver.

When we parted at the station in Cannes, Alexander kissed me on both cheeks and then, on second thoughts, hugged me warmly. 'The French don't approve of hugging unless you're a dog or a child,' he said. 'So this will have to last until we meet again, my dear.' He evidently imagines that I come from a place where warm embraces are commonplace. He gave me his telephone number and made me promise to get in touch soon and put him out of his misery concerning the 'situation'.

So here I am in the Carlton lobby, jittery with anticipation. From this vantage point, I have a good view of the brightly lit portico and the luxurious motor cars that pull up outside the hotel. It is really quite amusing to watch the doormen fly out to open the car doors as though the vehicle were on fire or the occupants giving birth but the folk who step out of those cars stroll into the hotel in the most leisurely way. It's hard to imagine why the panic apart from the obvious, that the privileged need wait for no man. Let alone a doorman.

I was almost overwhelmed by fatigue by the time the driver, a wiry, jockey-sized fellow, strode into the foyer and glared at me. '*Anglaise?*' Reading my startled expression as affirmative, he picked up my suitcase and with a flick of the head indicated that I should follow him. I was soon seated in the back of a smart black Citroen, being whisked out of Cannes and up the dark, twisting hills behind the city, all the while hoping he was my driver and not an opportunistic kidnapper. We drove through the streets of several villages and out into the darkness again and down winding country roads until he slowed to turn in through a set of wrought-iron gates at the entrance of Villa Rousseau.

As we pulled up outside the house the lights came on and Miss Brooke came out to welcome me. Let me dwell here for a moment so as not to skimp on my first impressions of my new employer. People often describe someone as 'once' having been a great beauty, which assumes that one must be young to achieve this sort of acclaim. But in Miss Brooke's case it seems possible that, in middle-age, she could be even more beautiful than in her youth. She possesses the sort of fine features and bone structure that may have once been merely pretty but a few decades of bedding in have resulted in a very pleasing effect. Her clothes are cut from the finest fabric, as is she. Her accent is less cutglass than sterling silver, the product of generations of 'good breeding'. But despite her smiling welcome and firm handshake, I caught a dark undercurrent of something complex: my best interpretation would be apprehension and mistrust; a stagnant decaying sort of odour like rotting leaves. It quite disoriented me for a moment. But she was kindness itself, expressing her concern at how exhausted I must be and her delight at my safe arrival. She guided me to my room, gesturing left and right to indicate various rooms (which I barely had time to take in) and then up three sets of stairs to the top level of the house, emphasising that I must make myself entirely at home – when I had never felt further away from that dear familiar place.

While the hallways and presumably the bedrooms we passed were rather sumptuous, this all ended abruptly on the third floor which is surprisingly dilapidated. I imagine this was once servants' quarters but she assured me I had the upper floor and the bathroom all to myself. It took some effort to disguise my disappointment when Miss Brooke opened the door to my room which is terribly shabby and spartan. Just an iron bedstead with white sheets. Not a rug or even a little vase to soften the effect. The only saving grace was a good-sized window with an old desk beneath it and the welcome sight of my trunk, which left London two weeks ago. The driver, whom Miss Brooke had introduced as Monsieur Lapointe, arrived with my suitcase which he placed at the end of the bed, leaving without a word. I was aware that this was not a form of subservience. There was plenty of time in the car to pick up the unmistakable smell of pure hostility. I have a high level of accuracy with this odour, which has an unpleasant ring to it, a bit like metal polish.

'You speak a little French – *oui*?' I struggled to think of a single word but Miss Brooke just shrugged and glanced around the drab little room with affection as though imagining all the good times I would experience here. A meal was offered, but my appetite had vanished and Miss Brooke bid me goodnight. Despite the lacklustre accommodation, as I sit here at the little desk, fresh from my bath and diligently recording the day, there is a vast sense of relief at having arrived in one piece. I feel almost intrepid.

Chapter Two

My eyes opened this morning to a different world. Not the thick grey dawn, the rumble of cars and trains and the dank smell of disappointment that permeates London these days – the heaviness of all that has come before in my beloved city.

My room was full of light and the early morning air chill but with a promise of warmth and sun. I dressed quickly and managed to find the kitchen again, a spacious and inviting room with a flagstone floor and long table laid with a single place. There was a pastry accompanied by two little pots, one of jam, the other of butter, and a glass of orange juice. A coloured woman in her mid-twenties, her long hair tied up in a blue scarf, walked in carrying a tray of crockery. She gave a brusque nod to indicate this place was set for me. Putting the tray down on the bench, she poured a cup of thick black coffee from a pot on the stove and placed it in front of me, her face blank, eyes avoiding mine. It was unnerving. Coffee is becoming fashionable in London now but not something I have ever wanted to try. I took a few sips to be polite but truly cannot see the

AMANDA HAMPSON

attraction in its black bitterness. I longed for a nice cup of tea but didn't dare ask.

Miss Brooke bustled in, dressed fetchingly in loose white trousers, a daffodil-yellow shirt and cream cardigan. She sent a warm smile in my direction. 'Good morning!' She then spoke in rapid French to the woman, who listened in silence as she methodically scrubbed each dish and stacked it on a wooden rack.

Miss Brooke turned her attentions to me. 'I hope you slept well, Iris. Ask Menna if you need anything.' I wanted to ask about my role but she was already halfway out the door, leaving Menna and myself in the depths of an uncomfortable silence only relieved by the clink of the dishes.

After breakfast I returned to my room and stood gazing out the window. My window looks out toward a rocky escarpment at the rear of the property. Directly below is a kitchen garden with rows of vegetables and a potting shed. I had that odd displacement you get when you don't belong somewhere and felt a longing for home and for my own tiny garden and the familiarity of everything around me. I had the sense of my little house in Linnet Lane waiting patiently for the sound of my key in the door. Not wanting to indulge my silly sentimentality, I went in search of Miss Brooke.

As I walked through the main vestibule with its checkerboard tiles, the sound of voices drew me toward an adjacent room. 'Who's that dazed little creature wandering about?' The man's voice was refined; drawn out with a sort of terminal lethargy. 'Looks ripe for the plucking.'

'She's the typist I had sent down from London for Hammond. Stay away from her,' Miss Brooke replied irritably.

'What does he want with a typist?' he asked.

Through the half-open door I glimpsed Miss Brooke sweeping about the room, industriously straightening magazines, fluffing cushions. 'What do you think, Jonathan?'

'Oh, his hocus-pocus? You're still plugging away at that old chestnut, are you?'

Satisfied with her endeavours, Miss Brooke made a beeline toward the door which called for a snap decision on my part. I tapped gently and popped my head around the door.

'Miss Turner! Do come in and meet Mr Fishell-Smith,' said Miss Brooke.

The man, middle-aged, thin and lanky, sat half reclined on the settee. He smoked languidly as he gazed out into the bright day through the open French doors, barely bothering to turn his head to see who had entered the room. I walked over and extended my hand self-consciously. He half rose to his feet and pressed his lips to the back of my hand.

'*Enchanté* – please, call me Jonathan. Fishell-Smith is such a dreadful mouthful.' He had a ruined smile and breath that would be dangerous near an open flame.

'Of course. I'm Iris . . . Miss Brooke's secretary.'

'We don't stand on ceremony here, my dear. Call her Vivian. She'd prefer that, so much more modern.' He collapsed loose-limbed back on the settee as though exhausted by the experience of being vertical.

'Of course, you must,' said Vivian stiffly. 'Jonathan is one of my most regular guests.'

'Spend more time here than I do at home, in fact,' he said, taking a long draw of his cigarette. He gave me a wan smile. 'Too many tiresome decisions to make at home. Here, darling Vivian makes them all for me.' He gazed longingly at Vivian. 'People often assume we were once lovers but, sadly, that was not the case — although there's still time to rectify that situation.'

'We're old friends,' said Vivian, shooting him a look. 'Family friends.' Changing tack, she opened her arms to embrace the room. 'This is my drawing room — isn't it splendid? Don't you adore it?'

I looked around, taking in the ostentatious antique furniture, crystal chandeliers, gloomy landscape paintings in ornate gilt frames, all set off by a heavily patterned wallpaper. The only aspect of real interest to me was an entire wall of books — floor-to-ceiling shelves with a moveable ladder on a rail. I was peripherally conscious of Jonathan's gaze upon me. He leaned forward abruptly. 'Viv, look at her, will you? Fresh as a peach.'

'Jonathan, that's enough — don't embarrass her,' said Vivian, scooping his ash off the Persian rug. But he had no plans to stop.

'Utterly enchanting! Would you like to come to England with me, my dear? I promise you'll never want for anything.'

I felt my cheeks glow. 'I'm afraid I am rather busy in the foreseeable future.'

He gave a splutter of laughter which turned into an uncontrollable coughing fit. Unamused, Vivian took my arm and led me out through the French doors. 'Needless to say, he has a wife, several former ones and countless children,' she said. 'Come and admire our view.' She led me across the tiled patio that runs the length of the house where large wicker chairs are arranged in clusters under the shade of a thick, twisted bougainvillea now sprouting scarlet blossoms, and then across the lawn to the terrace beyond.

That moment of walking out onto the terrace will remain with me forever. Having arrived at night, it wasn't evident just how elevated we are, perched high on the hill. Terraced gardens at the front of the villa drop sharply down to a valley and to green rolling hills that stretch all the way to a blue thread of the Mediterranean. The sky stretched forever into the distance, layer upon layer of blue. My body soaked up the milky warmth of the sun; it was as though I were emerging from years of hibernation. The air was dense with a salty sweetness. I discerned lavender, orange blossom, jasmine, roses – strawberries! I could even smell the rich earth from which they sprouted. Intoxicating scents.

Pleased by my obvious admiration, Vivian (it's so awkward having to use her Christian name, so I find myself avoiding any address) was inspired to take me on a rapid tour of the garden, through the rose bowery and past the swimming pool. She stopped at the orchard, the fruit trees now shedding their blossom for bright green leaves. She pointed out the guest cottage beyond and then, as if abruptly changing her mind, turned my attention back to the villa itself.

She apparently runs the place as a small exclusive hotel. There are eight bedrooms, five of which are renovated as guest rooms. It seems her guests come mainly from Britain, South Africa and the Far East. 'They come here to escape their dreary marriages or ghastly careers. It can be tiresome but I couldn't possibly afford to keep this place going without them.' Not once in the hour we spent together did she mention my role here. It was as though she has mistaken me for one of her guests.

We finally arrived back on the patio and before she could escape I asked if she could clarify my position and when I would commence work. 'Oh, I thought Mr Hubert explained the situation at the interview,' she said vaguely, now distracted by the appearance of the Citroen coming slowly down the driveway. Monsieur Lapointe had three passengers with several large trunks strapped to the roof. A taxi with even more trunks followed behind. Hurrying off to greet the new guests, Vivian suggested we meet in her office after lunch. So now I sit here pondering the possible meaning of 'Hammond and his hocus-pocus'.

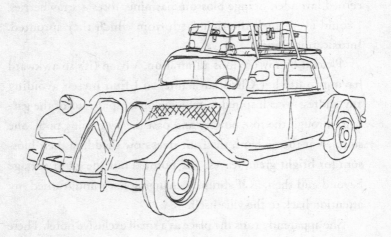

At lunchtime I made my way to the kitchen to find that Menna had disappeared but been replaced by a fierce little woman who was obviously the cook. She pointedly ignored me and there was no sign of lunch so I was at a bit of a loss until Vivian materialised and spoke to her. There was a terse exchange between them that seemed to end in a victory for the cook. This was confirmed when Vivian turned to me with a smile. 'You'll be dining with the guests while you're with us, Iris.'

'Oh really? I'd be far more comfortable here in the kitchen.'

She took my arm and led me down the hall. 'Madame Bouchard feels it beneath her to cook for staff, so it's better that you eat with us. Don't worry, we won't bite.'

The guests' luncheon is served at a long table in a beautiful conservatory, tastefully decorated with potted palms and Grecian statues, on the south side of the house. We were the last to arrive. The gentlemen rose gallantly from their seats upon our arrival and Jonathan made a point of welcoming me effusively and making introductions. He seems to have mastered the knack of maintaining a state of benign equanimity a couple of tipples short of pickled.

I was introduced to the new arrivals, Mr Douglas Farley and his much younger wife, who introduced herself as Lady Jessica. Mr Farley himself radiates affluence and arrogance but clearly dotes on the 'little woman' as an adored child. His flinty expression softened every time he looked her way which was usually to ascertain that she was not troubled by a lack of salt and pepper or similar culinary crisis. She is all Shirley Temple dimples and curls, displaying her tiny white teeth every time she laughs, which is often and invariably without cause.

The other more interesting new arrival is Mrs Somerville from New York. She is rather forbidding and seems given to introducing provocative topics in the hope of opening up a debate for which she has already formed her arguments and rebuttals – a woman in search of a worthy opponent, so it seems.

Mr Farley had brought the latest issue of *The Times* with him from London and there was discussion around the table about the growing hostilities between Egypt and Britain over the Suez Canal. He made the pompous pronouncement that Prime Minister Eden was a decent chap in whose diplomacy he had complete faith, which caused Mrs Somerville to issue forth a derisive snort. 'Eden!' she said. 'This is the guy who wanted to bargain with Hitler and Mussolini – right? You can't talk peace to dictators; if he'd had the guts right back at the start —'

Vivian stepped in. 'Mrs Somerville, more salad?'

Mr Farley responded icily. 'My dear woman, the war is over. And I for one have no desire to explore that particular subject any further.'

'Or that of Eden's digestive system, come to that,' added Jonathan affably.

'Well, you know Nasser is the Hitler of the Middle East,' Mrs Somerville said. 'If that fool of a prime minister of yours had any sense he'd believe Egypt's threats to obliterate Israel. Will Britain stand by and watch?'

'Are you Jewish yourself, Madam?' asked Mr Farley.

'Not at all, but many of my dearest friends —'

Like a knight preparing to joust, Mr Farley cast his wife a brave smile, tilted his lance and sallied forth. 'I'm not sure where you're getting your information, Mrs Somerville, but I assure you that neither the British Prime Minister nor the British people are fools – nor ignorant of complexities of foreign politics. The plight of the Israelites is hardly Britain's problem —'

Mrs Somerville opened her mouth to interject but was pipped by Jonathan. 'Splendid lunch as always, Viv.' He nodded encouragingly at the rest of us to follow suit and halt the escalation of hostilities.

Following his lead, Lady Jessica placed her hand on her husband's arm and asked sweetly, 'Mrs Somerville, I've been admiring your exquisite earrings. Are they amethysts?'

Ambushed by flattery, Mrs Somerville unclipped one of her

earrings and passed it to Lady Jessica who examined it with a practised eye and pronounced it superb. 'Have you seen Miss Kelly's engagement ring?' she asked in that confiding tone some women cultivate.

Mrs Somerville softened. 'Well, sure – she wore it in *High Society*, right?'

'Aren't you simply dying to see her bridal gown?' asked Lady Jessica.

'Ab-so-lutely!' said Mrs Somerville, leaning toward her new friend. 'I heard six seamstresses are working on it full-time.'

Mr Farley gave his young wife a look of admiration more commensurate with sorting out the Suez problem than a squabble at the tea table and added snootily, 'It's all just a public relations exercise for the Americans.'

Ignoring him, Mrs Somerville turned to Lady Jessica. 'Are you and Mr Farley invited?'

Her ladyship trilled with laughter. 'Heavens, no, but we plan to be outside St Nicholas Cathedral when she leaves as Princess Grace. Do come with us, won't you?'

'According to the papers, the driver will take their Highnesses on a tour of Monte Carlo, so everyone can catch a glimpse,' said Vivian. 'Although I can't say I'm terribly interested.'

'I wouldn't miss it for the world!' said Mrs Somerville, as though taking umbrage at Vivian's ambivalence toward the occasion which, quite honestly, does seem to have the whole world in a thrall. To give Lady Jessica her due, peace reigned and it was indeed a very nice lunch with tomatoes, peppery lettuce, string beans, ham and chicken. Pudding was a rich buttery pastry with custard and strawberries – quite a feast for the middle of the day.

Lunch over, it seemed we would finally get down to business. Vivian has a lovely little 'salon' where she presides at a splendidly ornate desk centred to the room with two upright antique chairs facing it. It was a little intimidating – you could imagine finding yourself sitting in one of these rather uncomfortable chairs being hauled over the coals. (I hope that is an idle thought, and not a premonition.) She had the lovely smiling maid, Amandine, who had waited on us at lunch, bring us both a nice cup of tea which quite revived me.

'I do apologise for keeping you in the dark for so long,' Vivian said, sipping her tea. 'I wanted to get a better sense of your character before I fully entrusted you with this position.' I was intrigued by the admission that she had purposely kept me in the dark. Did she also mean I could have been rejected at this stage and sent home? Surely not!

'I can see you're an honest and, I hope, trustworthy person. You don't talk for the sake of it. This role calls for the utmost discretion. You need to give me your solemn promise that you will not discuss any aspect of your job – even the nature of your job – with anyone other than myself.' Although mystified, I assured her of my complete discretion.

'You will be working for my brother, Mr Hammond Brooke, who lives in the guest cottage you saw at the far end of the garden. Your hours will be 10 a.m. to 1 p.m. with an hour for lunch and a further hour for rest. Then work will recommence from 3 p.m. to 6 p.m., at which point you can freshen up and join myself and the guests for dinner at 8 p.m.'

'And the nature of the work?'

'Mr Brooke is almost blind. At the moment he can distinguish light and dark, shapes, etcetera, but he will eventually be in complete darkness. He has some things —' she paused to select the right phrase — 'some elements of his work, that need to be recorded and his affairs put in order.'

'I understand.'

'I think it's preferable to treat you as our guest here because, as you will have observed, my staff speak no English and your French is evidently limited. You'd find yourself very isolated and possibly want to leave. I can't prevent you leaving but I would be very disappointed if you did so before this project was completed.'

'I can't see any reason why I wouldn't see it through,' I assured her.

'You will need to be extremely discreet. If you reveal that you are working with my brother to the likes of Her Ladyship or Mrs Somerville, you'll find yourself under scrutiny – which may make things awkward for us all. Jonathan is aware of the situation but please don't discuss it with him.' I found myself nodding stupidly at this complicated explanation.

'My brother does not care for visitors. He does not want to be the subject of curiosity or even a topic of conversation among guests here. We value our privacy above all else.'

With growing trepidation, my gaze was drawn to the open window where the sheer curtain fluttered on the breeze, revealing glimpses of the garden and, beyond the orchard, the cottage.

'Do you understand?' she asked.

'What if guests see me going to or from the cottage – what should I say?'

She looked at me as though now having doubts. 'They mustn't see you, obviously. You are simply another guest here.'

Despite my confusion, I continued to nod agreeably.

'You can rest today and start tomorrow morning.'

'Do I simply arrive there at ten?' I asked.

'Yes, he's aware you're here. He's expecting you.' Vivian rose from her seat. 'We're very glad to have you here.' I took that as my cue to thank her and leave.

After the meeting, I came back to my room to sit down and think and write. There is a drowsiness in the air and the house is quite silent apart from the sound of intermittent snoring in the distance somewhere, perhaps the room below. I will need to do some reconnaissance to work out how to get to the cottage unobserved from the house. It seems ridiculous that this is a necessary part of the job but don't want to find myself, as Vivian implied, a source of interest nor to be cross-examined – let alone by Mrs Somerville! I am looking forward to ending this period of limbo and actually starting work.

I'm back from my mission. While everyone napped, I went downstairs and wandered around the terraced gardens but the house has a dress-circle view of these gardens. I walked around to the back of the house to the kitchen garden I can see from my bedroom window. At the rear of the building there are stairs leading down to a rather sinister-looking cellar, perhaps where the wine is kept as the windows are all barred. Beyond the garden is the rock face. I walked up the driveway and located the track running parallel with the rock face and was able to follow it all the way across the width of the property. The path then continued further up the hill, perhaps a short cut to the road, but the bank itself sloped gently into the garden behind the cottage, so this will be quite satisfactory.

That task completed, I am back in my room reunited with my notebook, my only friend and confidant in this strange – and growing stranger – place. Soon I must prepare for dinner. I almost never dine out and have so few suitable clothes. Normally the highlight of my evening is listening to *The Archers* and 7 p.m. news by which time I have had my supper, popped into my pyjamas and curled up in the armchair with Mitzi on my lap. That all seems a million miles away. And nothing can ever be the same. Mitzi is gone and there is now a worrying development in the wind that I haven't wanted to think about.

My last conversation with Alan was profoundly disappointing. I had arranged to meet him for a farewell drink a few days before I left. From the moment my dear brother arrived, there was a sense that he had been allotted limited time and was channelling his bossy wife, Ruth, even borrowing her trademark expressions; for example, adding 'as such' to the end of a sentence, a phrase she utilises to soften a blow or underline her latest edict.

Glancing at his watch, he murmured about plans to move to a larger house in a better part of Kingston so the children had more room to run around. I managed to resist suggesting they could use a little restraining – they show off in the most precocious manner. What he was explaining was, that although he had so far protected me from Ruth's avaricious claims on our family home, since I would be away for a period, it was a 'perfect' opportunity to sell the property and split the proceeds which would allow his family to move up a rung or two on the social ladder. *As such.* I reminded him that Father had made it clear he wanted me to be able to continue to live in our home until I married or some less desirable fate befell me. But he shrugged helplessly.

I am resisting this strenuously not only because it's our family home but because I won't be able to afford another house on half the funds. Alan and Ruth have an extremely comfortable detached house in Kingston; they may have a mortgage but at least they are eligible for one – no bank would lend money to an unmarried woman.

I've been aware for some time that it's better not to remind Ruth of my existence but I do love to see Alan. His presence is such a comfort to me. The last time I was invited to their home was for his birthday, a few months after Father passed away. It was a party of sorts, rather uncomfortable as most people seemed associated with his work and I knew no one apart from his family. I had several glasses of unpleasantly sweet white wine and, unused to alcohol, immediately felt a little woozy. I sobered up quickly when I overheard Ruth – who also can't hold her liquor, it seems – telling a guest that Alan was hopelessly unbusinesslike. Very disloyal of her, I thought, and untrue – he's a solicitor, for goodness sake! She explained that he had allowed his sister to remain in the family home. 'His sister is terribly selfish.' She glanced around but still didn't notice me standing nearby. 'She could easily live in a little flat somewhere. It's just her and a dreadful old cat.'

It was the 'dreadful old cat' that upset me more than anything else.

Ruth enjoys a heated argument which apparently 'clears the air' but Alan and I grew up in a household where speaking up could have disastrous consequences, so our natural instinct is to slip away and wait for things to sort themselves out. That evening at the pub, this worked in my favour and the promise that I would think about it was enough for Alan to down his pint, deliver an awkward one-armed hug and lumber off into the night. I am well aware that's not the end of it, though. The minute Ruth decides to charge ahead with her plans, Alan will be dragged along behind.

Dinner this evening was in the formal dining room, all very grand, decorated and embellished at every turn. Two huge chandeliers are suspended over the polished oak dining table which was beautifully laid with white linen and copious heavy silver cutlery and glasses at every setting.

It is all terribly elegant but I have begun to observe that, although the icing on this cake is impressive, beneath it there are signs of decay. Behind strategically placed furnishings can be seen cracks in the wall, the odd patching here and there, and during my reconnaissance this afternoon I noticed the smell of sewage, leaking perhaps from broken pipes behind the house. I'm wondering if Vivian is in something of a bind. It seems to me that she is struggling to woo these wealthy guests with the best of everything but the house is quietly disintegrating around her – before she has even finished renovating it.

It was a bit of a shock this evening to discover that guests 'dress' for dinner; men in tuxedos, Vivian resplendent in a navy floor-length silk gown with a diamond and pearl necklace. So much for not standing on ceremony! I felt terribly out of place in my black wool, and certainly no one would mistake my paste brooch for diamonds. It is a preposterous idea that anyone would believe I am a guest here; one can only imagine the tariffs that provide for this level of luxury.

Thankfully the evening meal was an altogether quieter affair, less combative than lunch, partly as the result of a new guest. Just as we commenced our soup course a rather dashing gentleman, whom Vivian introduced as Mr Geraldson, arrived. He apologised briefly for his late arrival and sat down at a place that had been laid for him. Although not in uniform, his posture and presence were that of a commanding officer, borne out by the fact that everyone seemed to snap to attention when he appeared. Mr Farley placed his arm protectively along the back of his wife's chair. Jonathan gave Geraldson a courteous, if indifferent, nod. It would seem they are previously acquainted. Strangely, although he was seated next to me, I had no sense of him – he gave out nothing but coldness. Clearly a man of great emotional control, no inkling of his internal state seeps from his pores.

Vivian had shrewdly seated Mr Farley and Mrs Somerville at diametrically opposite corners of the table which placed Mr Geraldson directly across from Mrs Somerville. She eyed him with suspicion. As her spoon moved from bowl to mouth in a steady rhythm, there was a predatory alertness about her.

Vivian brightly suggested that Monsieur Lapointe could take anyone who would like to go on an excursion into the nearby town of Grasse for market day on Saturday. Jonathan, seated on my other side, thought this a grand idea. He snatched up my hand and pressed it to his florid cheek, gazing at me with blood-shot eyes. 'I hope my young bride-to-be will join me.'

Everyone, apart from Vivian, turned to stare at me. 'He's joking,' I assured them, reclaiming my hand. 'We just met this morning.'

'This morning? It feels like a lifetime ago,' Jonathan sighed.

Judging by her expression, I am certain Vivian feels – as do I – that this silly pantomime has already gone on too long.

Although I could hardly be described as a 'woman of the world', if nothing else, seventeen years in the civil service has to some extent prepared me for men like Jonathan. When I was younger, my resistance to making a fuss made me easy quarry. For years I tolerated suggestive comments, pats on the bottom and worse in polite silence. Transgressions ignored simply emboldened another more daring infringement on my person. If anything it got worse as I got older. Some of my colleagues seemed to think I would be grateful for a clumsy grope. Making a fuss often had a habit of backfiring and over the years several girls left the department to escape unfairly damaged reputations. Eventually I discovered that deflecting this type of behaviour with tact and firm good humour somehow defused the situation. I do hope that a day in Grasse will alleviate Jonathan's boredom and give him something else to focus his attentions on.

I'm quite nervous about meeting Mr Brooke tomorrow. Even more so now that I realise he is not only blind but something of a recluse. I don't believe Vivian is being deliberately obtuse or mysterious – probably the last thing she wants to do is to pique my curiosity. I'm almost certain there is an impending crisis that she is desperately trying to avert.

Chapter Three

Today started well enough, then it all got horribly complicated. Most guests seem to rise closer to lunchtime than breakfast, so it was a simple matter to slip out of the house undetected. I set off with my stenographer's notebook and pencil tucked in my handbag, my tummy roiling with nervous anticipation. I followed the track behind the trees, arriving in the back garden of the cottage as planned. Monsieur Lapointe and another man, whom I took to be Mr Brooke, sat out on chairs in the sun. Pungent smoke from their cigarettes lingered in the still morning air. Monsieur Lapointe saw me approach through the garden and alerted Mr Brooke, who turned in my direction.

'It's Miss Turner, sir! Good morning!' I called out as though he were actually deaf. And when he didn't respond, added helpfully, 'Your secretary!'

He gave a harsh laugh. 'What the bloody hell would I want with a secretary?'

'You are Mr Brooke?'

'How many blind Englishmen do you think there are in

Grasse?' he asked.

'Of course, I do apologise.'

Monsieur Lapointe stood and stretched. He murmured to Mr Brooke, who nodded, seemingly irritated that their conversation had been interrupted. He laid his hand on Mr Brooke's shoulder in a gesture that spoke less of an employee's regard than of something more resonant; a comradeship, perhaps. I stood there awkwardly and watched Monsieur Lapointe walk through the orchard to the house, wishing I could follow.

'Who's up at the house now?' Mr Brooke asked tersely.

'Oh, ah, Mrs Somerville, Mr Farley and Lady Jessica —'

'Geraldson?'

'Yes, Mr Geraldson arrived last night.'

'It's no coincidence that bastard's here,' he fumed.

'I am sorry, sir. I'm confused. I understood —' Approaching him I picked up on the acrid fume of bitterness, which I have come to believe is more acidic than pure anger. His particular bitterness was complex, mixed with something else that ran counter; possibly a deep sense of despair.

'Vivian's set you up, girl.' He gave a grunt of amusement. 'A blind date.'

'I don't understand —'

'No. I wouldn't expect you to.' He rubbed the stubble on his face thoughtfully. It's not immediately obvious that he is blind, but it's soon evident in that he doesn't look directly at you but in the vicinity. He has been a striking man in his youth but now in his fifties, hair grizzled grey, features craggy, he looks worn out, like a stately building fallen into disrepair. 'What did you say your name was?'

I took this as an invitation to slip onto the chair beside him.

'Miss Turner, Sir. Iris Turner.'

'Iris. Messenger of the gods.' He pondered that for a moment and, a trifle less hostile, asked, 'And do you have a message for me, Iris Turner?'

'From the underworld?'

He gave a bark of laughter. 'This is the underworld, Miss Turner. And now you're trapped here with the other damned souls.' He closed his eyes and raised his face to meet the sun. 'Who's idea was it?'

'Idea? There was an advertisement —'

'The name. Iris. You obviously know your Greek mythology.'

'My father was a school teacher; he taught ancient history. My brother was to be named Asopus but my mother won the day with Alan.'

He laughed. We fell silent for a few moments and then he said, 'Tell me what you see in this garden of mine, Iris Turner.'

This part of the property is at the end of a wide plateau after which the land falls away gradually, tapering into the hillside. To the south is the view down the valley to the sea. The dense garden surrounding the cottage is a riot of spring flowers, planted higgledy-piggledy like an English cottage garden: violets, daffodils, irises, poppies, primrose, lily-of-the-valley, all muddled together. I enumerated these to Mr Brooke, who nodded as though in time to a musical beat, occasionally interrupting me to ask if the crocus had flowered or if the gold tulips were in bloom.

'What did Vivian tell you?' he asked.

'Simply that I would be working for you. That you had some aspects of your work that you needed recording.'

He pulled a packet of French cigarettes from his shirt pocket and, in a seamless action, selected one with his lips, exchanged the pack for a lighter, lit up and inhaled deeply. 'What else do you know? About my work?'

'Nothing but I . . . I overheard Jonathan referring to it as your "hocus-pocus".' I don't know why I blurted that out, perhaps in the hope of making him laugh – making him like me a bit more. But it had the opposite effect. He expelled an angry plume of smoke.

'Don't tell me that bloody idiot's still here. How long's he staying?'

'I'm really not privy to that sort of information. I'm not a guest.'

'And you don't speak French, I hear. That would suit Vivian very nicely. What else are they talking about up at the house?'

I mentioned the forthcoming wedding of Grace Kelly and Prince Rainier as a major topic in the London papers Mr Farley had brought. He emitted that contemptuous expulsion of breath the French do so well. I added that there had been discussion about Suez and he asked me about the mood in England; whether people realised the potential impact on Britain. Not being an arbiter of public opinion, I cast around for a suitably non-partisan response. I had listened to my father's politically biased commentary – which sometimes bounced off the walls – all my life and had in the past made the mistake of parroting his opinions in the outside world with catastrophic results. These days I cultivate a position of neutrality.

I asked Mr Brooke how long it had been since he was in England. He said several years prior to the war and he had no desire to go back now. Despite that, he listens to the BBC World Service regularly and is much better informed than myself. We got into a general discussion during which I seemed to be holding my own when, quite to my surprise, he got up, announced he was tired and walked off toward the cottage. He guided himself confidently, touching the back of the chair lightly, tapping his foot to locate the edge of the terrace, and found the door without hesitation.

'Mr Brooke, what about the work?'

'Don't tell me your troubles, Miss Turner. I expect you have worked out by now that I didn't employ you.' He walked inside and shut the door. It was barely 11.30 a.m. I had no idea what on earth to do. What to tell Vivian? My spirits lifted briefly as the door reopened. 'If she doesn't send you packing, you can visit again.'

'Tomorrow?'

'If you must. And bring those newspapers.' He stood at the door waiting for me to leave, well aware that I was still standing there, but I seemed to be rooted to the spot. 'I'm not a guest here either, Miss Turner. I'm a prisoner,' he said. Then the door slammed hard.

As luck would have it, Monsieur Lapointe took Vivian and the Farleys to Nice this morning and they won't return until early evening. I have managed to remain inconspicuous this afternoon, although Menna has seen me. She never uses the main stair but appears and disappears, silent as a shadow, via the back service stair. There is nowhere to hide from her all-seeing gaze. She knows I was home mid-morning and didn't return to the cottage. The question is, will she tell Vivian? Should I tell Vivian that I don't have Mr Brooke's cooperation? I can't decide. A frank admission from me would be better than a report from someone else. But what if she sends me home? Having turned my back on 'home and hearth' to gallop off on my 'little adventure' (as it became condescendingly referred to in the department) and then limp back a week later would be mortifying.

Dinner this evening was excruciating. Knowing Vivian likes to be punctual with meals, I timed my arrival to the minute to avoid being alone with her but came downstairs to find her titivating the floral arrangement in the vestibule. She dropped all floral aspirations as soon as she saw me and enquired as to the progress today. I tried not to appear evasive, explaining that there had been some discussion, we had not started work as yet, but would do so in the morning.

While she can be extremely charming and convivial, there is another side to her which is quite intimidating. There are long pauses and awkward moments while her mistrustful side silently assesses information. It is as though she's giving you space to blurt the truth – which plays on my particular weakness. On this occasion, however, she seemed to accept my story. 'Don't let him procrastinate. He knows this has to be done, and with some urgency. If he won't cooperate, then make him walk. He needs to exercise.' With that, she hurried into the dining room to soothe her guests, all of whom were out of sorts for a variety of reasons.

Jonathan had apparently fallen asleep on a sun lounge (amusing himself with a bottle or two of wine, no doubt) and appeared at dinner with a wretched hangover, his face a livid shade of rosé.

It has come to light that our resident lovebirds, Mr Farley and Lady Jessica, are actually on their honeymoon, but tonight they sat side by side wearing identical sullen expressions. I had an insight into this as I had been in my room when the party returned from Nice. I heard the door below me slam hard and soon became aware of a ruckus: raised voices, footsteps running back and forth, heavy objects hitting the walls – a domestic disturbance that clearly had not been resolved.

Mrs Somerville's nose was thoroughly out of joint and she made several pointed comments about being *stranded* here all day with no driver and that she would very much have liked to visit Nice *herself* had the invitation been extended to her. Vivian soothed her with apologies and promises of inclusion in future excursions.

Mr Geraldson, of more interest since his presence engendered such fury in Mr Brooke, did not involve himself. In fact, he does not involve himself full stop. Immersed in the meal in front of him, he could be eating alone. Although at one point during Mrs Somerville's lament, he glanced across at Vivian with an expression of blatant annoyance, presumably at her failure to immediately placate the woman.

In a craven effort to curry favour with Vivian, I took it upon myself to engage both Mrs Somerville and Jonathan in conversation. But holding court is not my strength and the conversation quickly withered and died. As the evening staggered to a close, Lady Jessica's curls suddenly flopped forwards of their own accord, concealing her face. Her chin rested on her chest and in the puzzled silence that followed she could be heard snoring quite charmingly like a child. There is copious wine at dinner, although I never touch it, but she had been drinking in a quietly determined way all evening and was likely stewed. Her embarrassed husband tried to rouse her and, when that failed, attempted to lift her bodily out of her chair. But she was as floppy as a ragdoll and it took both Mr Farley and Mr Geraldson to carry her upstairs – needless to say, not in a terribly dignified manner.

I gathered up her little velvet purse and cashmere wrap, which had fallen to the floor, and followed them upstairs. It was my first excursion into one of the guest rooms and, once inside, I was hit by the peppery odour associated with friction and discord. The room is quite grand, all silvers and greys, dominated by an elaborate cream bedroom suite in baroque or rococo style. The walls feature an overwrought wallpaper pattern similar to that of downstairs; this one adorned with peacocks and palm trees. The Farleys had obviously not been expecting visitors. It seems the hurried footsteps had been a pitched battle in which every possible item had been hurled across the room, presumably at the other party. Mr Geraldson, whose usual expression lends the term impassive another dimension, stared around in wonderment at the sheer scale of disarray.

The two men placed Her Ladyship on the bed where she lay like a helpless little bird in the nest of satin and lace lingerie flung there. She has a penchant for pretty shoes and these were now spread all over the room but I noticed she was only wearing one of her black velvet slippers topped with the pink silk tearoses. I ducked downstairs and found it under the table. On the way back up I passed Mr Geraldson on the stairs; he looked quietly amused.

I knocked gently at the Farleys' door. Hearing no answer, I assumed Mr Farley was tending to his wife or had perhaps gone to the bathroom which is accessed from the hall. Opening the door slightly, I bent down to slip the shoe just inside and was struck by a palpable stillness in the room and the fermenting odour of resentment in the air. I glanced up to see Mr Farley kneeling on the bed at his wife's feet, unbuckling his belt. I felt a rush of protective fury that he would take advantage of her while she was comatose – or perhaps because she was comatose! One moment the shoe was in my hand and the next it was hurtling across the room toward the back of his head. I heard him grunt as I quickly pulled the door closed. In a blind panic, I opened the nearest door and threw myself inside. Needless to say, when I set off this morning with such high hopes, I did not expect to end the day hiding in a linen hamper having assaulted a paying guest.

Before the house awoke this morning, I gathered all the newspapers I could find and took them across to the cottage. I spent the morning sitting in the sun with Mr Brooke and reading *The Times* aloud. He made the odd comment or grunt here and there. On and on it went and I knew another day would pass without any progress. Finally, I put my foot down. 'Sir, perhaps we should go for a walk.'

'Oh, for Christ's sake, stop calling me "Sir"!'

I felt myself becoming quiet and small – as I had learned to deal with Father's outbursts – and struggled to shake this feeling as I listened to Mr Brooke explain at some length that, unlike the main house, his house was classless, egalitarian. He couldn't stand all the hobnobbing and kowtowing that went on up there. 'It's the last bloody bastion of the British empire. Fools with titles and money. Fascists. Self-satisfied bourgeoisie.'

'You might then be interested to know that my father was a Marxist,' I said in a bid to align myself with his ideology.

'Was?'

'He died last year. Still a Marxist.'

'I was apolitical before the war. I enjoyed a privileged life, had no need of politics. The war changed all that. I don't know

what I would call myself now. I'd like to think I'm a humanist.'
We sat in the stillness of the day, lulled by the sun and the low
hum of bees going about their business in the garden. 'Did he
fight in Spain?' he asked.

'My father? No. I suppose he was an armchair activist, a
vocal observer and commentator of the Spanish war. Besides, the
Somme left him unfit for active duty. His gas mask was punc-
tured by a bullet. The gas leaked in and burnt the side of his jaw
and affected his lungs.'

'He was lucky to survive that,' he said.

'I'm not sure he always saw it that way.' I folded up the newspaper briskly as if to imply it was time to get on with some work.

'And your mother?' he asked.

I sighed. Partly at the mention of my mother, but mostly
because there seemed to be no end to his determination to
create interminable delays and distractions. The sun was now
high in the sky. I was hungry and tired after a restless night worrying about the potential repercussions of my assault on Mr Farley.
'It's a long story but, if you're interested, I could tell you when
I come back this afternoon.'

'Anything to alleviate the boredom of my existence,' he said
gloomily, but I felt quite pleased at having deftly engineered a
return visit.

It has just now dawned on me that Vivian knows perfectly
well that her brother doesn't want me here and that he has no
plans to cooperate. She's waiting to see if I can bridge his resistance. All I can do right now is play for time. Somehow, I have to
make this work. I am nothing if not persistent.

———

When Mr Farley appeared for lunch, I noticed a slight pinkness at the top of his ear. Nothing wrong with my bowling arm! I doubt there was much force behind the blow. It simply clipped him in a tender spot. No regrets on my part, especially since I am almost certain now that he won't make a complaint, although he must suspect me since Mr Geraldson is hardly the shoe-hurling type.

We all sat down to an overly rich casserole with copious onions and beans and it was as though nothing untoward had occurred the evening before. Everyone behaved perfectly. This is one of the joys of being British; discretion is our national strength. Averse to any sort of awkwardness, it comes quite naturally to us to pretend all is well. Nothing has changed. Unless I am misreading this and unconscious guests are regularly hefted up the stairs?

However, my opinion of Mr Farley has undergone a complete reversal. I had accepted his superior ways as a prerogative of his class but it is now clear that his attentiveness to his wife is less an expression of adoration than a means to control her. I now see that the poor woman can barely lift a finger, let alone offer an opinion, without his interference. He has a repertoire of subtle glances and expressions; a tiny questioning frown that makes her hesitate; an infinitesimal shake of the head that makes her falter. Perhaps she enjoyed his attentions initially but I now see a tension in her that I didn't notice before. Her pointless laughter is a nervous reaction; there's a slight desperation in her pearly smile. One senses that they haven't known each other terribly long.

Vivian and most of the guests observe a rest period after lunch, although it's difficult to imagine that they could possibly need any more rest. I am not in the habit of napping and today have brought my journal to the drawing room despite the slight risk of running into Jonathan, given this is where the drinks trolley resides. Despite its ostentation, I do like this room. The library beckons with a vista of possibilities and, if I can hold on to my position here, I hope to take full advantage. What a comfort to wander the length of the shelves, to caress the spines of old friends – Jane Austen, Thomas Hardy, George Eliot – and endeavour to make the acquaintance of new ones. True nourishment for my soul.

I also plan to brush up on my pitiful French. I was sadly disadvantaged by the fact that our French teacher, the tyrannical Mrs Barker, didn't care for the language (or the French themselves, for that matter) nor speak it. So lessons were dreary rotes of verb conjugations from recordings that made no sense at all to us. I am starting to recognise words I hear regularly and will try to make a note of these and check the spelling and meaning in my French–English Dictionary. One word at a time.

Yesterday finished disastrously, infinitely worse than the previous evening.

I had been back at Mr Brooke's at precisely 3 p.m. I felt it important to continue to be businesslike and professional, although that has completely flown out the window now. As I made my way to the cottage, dark clouds hung low overhead. There was a brisk breeze and flecks of rain stung my cheeks. While my past visits have found Mr Brooke in the garden, today I would cross his threshold for the first time and must confess I was very curious. I knocked at the door and waited. He's so mercurial, I half expected him to shout at me to go away but he called out to come in.

Stepping into the house, I was assaulted by a veritable cascade of smells. It was as though every flower in the world had come here to die, the fragrances composted and fermented, distilled down into a dense rancidity that was absorbed through my every pore, so overpowering that I could barely breathe.

'Are you planning to stand sentry all afternoon?' he asked. 'Sit down, for God's sake.'

I sat in the armchair opposite him and glanced around at the clutter. Hundreds of books tumbling from shelves, dozens of paintings, some hung and others stacked against the walls. Artefacts in brass and copper, perhaps from North Africa, and piles and piles of papers, none of which he could see any more. The house is an obstacle course completely unsuited to a blind person, yet clearly he is intimately acquainted with this terrain and can navigate his way, even in his darkness.

'What is that . . . strange . . . odour?' I asked.

'Odour?' His tone was scathing. 'If you mean smell, why don't you just come right out with it?'

'All right, what is the queer smell?'

'What do you smell?' he asked.

'Frustration,' I said before I could stop myself.

That gave him pause for thought. He tilted his nose and drew in a long measured breath, explored that breath at some length and exhaled in a dismissive burst. 'Did any more papers arrive?'

'No, and no new guests either.'

'Geraldson left yet?'

'He's still there. He seems to be enjoying himself a little more.'

'Enjoying himself!' he spluttered. 'What the hell are you talking about?'

Having further infuriated him, I found myself telling the story of Lady Jessica falling into drunken stupor (phrased more delicately) and Mr Geraldson's role in helping carry her upstairs, but naturally left out the entire shoe-throwing incident.

Mr Brooke asked what I knew of Mr Farley, a name he thought familiar. I have gleaned a few pieces of information. He appears to be in banking and has on occasion referred to his London house and an estate in Dorset. He is always evasive about anything related to the war, so his rank and where he served (of keen interest to Mr Brooke) has not been revealed. Warming to the subject, I described his character and relationship with his wife in some detail. In my experience, males are seldom interested in minute observations of another's character – they want to know what a man does and who his family are – but Mr Brooke was very attentive. He was determined to know Farley's connection with Vivian but I couldn't work out quite what he was alluding to – whether he thought the man had some kind of history with Vivian or if he was a business associate of some sort. He hinted that I could possibly find that information out.

'Are you suggesting that I spy on guests and report back to you?'

'It may not be quite how Vivian envisioned it – but it would be useful, yes.'

'She's going to ask me what we did today and I am almost certain that gossiping about guests is not what she wants to hear.'

'Try not to think of it as gossip,' he said. 'More as reconnaissance.'

It was raining heavily outside now. The wind gusted against the house, rattling windows, and the room had grown dim. Although only the middle of the afternoon, outside it was twilight.

'Look at the bright side. You're in here talking to me. That's more than the others managed,' he said.

'Others?'

He swiftly changed the subject. 'Let's have a drink.' I made it clear that daytime drinking is not something I indulge in, but offered to get him one.

'There's a box near the door,' he said. 'Bring two glasses. And turn some lights on. I can't see a damn thing.'

I did as he asked and found the box which contained half-a-dozen bottles of red wine that I reluctantly brought over with the two glasses. I had a sinking feeling that this was another of his delaying tactics and would eat up what was left of the day. He had me take each bottle out and read the label aloud, to which he said yes or no. I brought him a corkscrew and he deftly opened one and poured two glasses of wine, his finger delicately tipped just over the rim to prevent spillage. Throughout the process, he acted, as he always does, as though fully sighted. He does ask to be handed or passed things but more as a convenience, to save himself the bother. To do all this with only shadows to guide him seems extraordinary to me.

He proffered an almost full glass and I really had no choice but to take it. 'Tell me what you can smell,' he said. He lit a cigarette and leaned back in his chair as though preparing to be entertained.

I breathed in, first short and gentle and then long and deep as I had seen him do earlier. 'Soil . . . wood . . . chalk . . .'

'No, go deeper, beyond the literal. Find the tones.'

I tried again, closed my eyes and allowed the smells to flood my senses. 'Nutmeg?' I ventured. 'Cloves.'

'Yes, continue,' he said impatiently.

'Exactly how many secretaries have you had?'

'What? Just a couple – perhaps three or four. Never mind about that. What else?'

'Pepper.'

'Nice,' he said. 'Now take a small mouthful, hold it in your mouth and draw some air through it. What do you taste?'

'Berries?'

He took a swig of his wine and laughed. 'Nutmeg; berries!' he snorted. 'You were right the first time. Earth and grapes – peasant pee. Vivian keeps the decent stuff up at the house. You've got a good imagination, I'll give you that.'

In fact, it tasted rank and bitter as ink to me, red wine having never touched my lips before. Hot with humiliation, I took an angry gulp. 'So were your previous secretaries also subjected to these games?'

'Silly little things. Brainless debutantes sired by Vivian's expat pals, scourge of the Côte d'Azur. Hardly worth the effort.'

'So why am I still here?' Holding back hot tears, each gulp increased my recklessness incrementally. We were going nowhere. I had nothing to lose.

He pondered the question. 'You're observant.'

'What does that mean?'

'Miss Turner, in case you haven't noticed, I'm *blind*.'

Rather than feeling chastised, presumably his strategy, the way he played his blindness as a trump card had the opposite effect on me. Vivian wants me to record something that he doesn't want to divulge. He wants me to spy on her and her guests. They are both so determined. She pushes forward, he sidesteps and, when cornered, uses his blindness as a foil.

'I'm sorry if you were offended by my little prank,' he said, sounding not at all contrite.

I drained the glass. The taste did not improve but the jangling in my head had given way to gliding moments of clarity and insight. 'I'm not sure you are sorry. I think you've rather enjoyed making a fool of me.'

'I need to get my amusement where I can,' he admitted.

He settled back in his chair smugly and sipped his wine. The blankness in his gaze is unnerving and I could feel myself going over the edge of boldness into a place from which there would be no coming back.

'I left my home and job to come here because —' I stopped myself. I didn't want to reveal anything he could use against me.

'Yes?' He wore the expression of a man who enjoys playing the upper hand.

'Because I wanted to prove something.'

'So what part do I play in this little experiment of yours, Miss Turner?'

'— and now I feel like a complete fool.'

His evident amusement at my upset was making me furious. I tried to get up but the chair was somehow lower to the floor than when I sat down. Extricating myself was more difficult than anticipated. The room swayed gently.

'Sit down, girl. You're overreacting now. What are you talking about? No one takes you for a fool.'

I picked my way carefully to the door.

'Come back. Sit down. You're being ridiculous.'

There was a splinter of something in his voice but I was in no state to analyse it then. I was too deep in the realisation that my situation here was untenable. As I walked out into the blustering rain, I envisioned Monsieur Lapointe taking me to the train, my arrival back in Linnet Lane, Ruth amusing guests with the story of her hapless sister-in-law and, worst of all, the disappointment of my dearest friend, Colleen, who had urged me on this journey. It was more than I could bear and I was seized by a kind of blind terror.

Next thing I was stumbling through the orchard. Wind and rain whipped around me. Then I was on my knees, wine gushing up my throat, making its way back into the earth. Then strong, gentle hands lifted me up, helped me back to my room and out of my wet, muddy clothes, mopped my face with a wet cloth, held a glass of cold water to my lips and tucked a blanket tightly around me as though I were a child. And I slept.

I woke this morning feeling raw, angry, defiant – perhaps even a little fearless. Hardly the way I would have expected to feel, given my disgraceful behaviour last night. I can't bear to think of it. That moment when I was so wretched, on my knees in every sense, rekindled a childhood memory. I was perhaps eight or nine and with my friend at the local baths. In a moment of spiteful fun she pushed me into the deep end, knowing full well I couldn't swim. I vividly remember sinking to the bottom of the pool, the air dragged from my lungs. I was too surprised to react but when my knees felt the hard surface beneath me, I somehow found the strength to push myself up toward the light, thrashing my way to the surface where someone plucked me from the pool. Although technically it was Menna who saved me last night, I am reminded of my own strength to endure perhaps more than I imagine.

My first thought is to pack my suitcase, explain the situation to Vivian and go home. It sounds simple enough in theory but the prospect of finding my way home is extremely daunting. To arrive here, there had been a list of detailed instructions. The hotel in Paris was reserved, the train booked. To undertake that journey in reverse, alone and with so little of the language, is terrifying. The thought makes me feel queasy. Or perhaps that's the aftermath of that ghastly wine.

Chapter Four

A wonderful day – I hardly know where to start!

I didn't realise when I woke this morning in such a gloomy frame of mind that overnight the world around me has inexplicably become more hospitable. Menna arrived at my door bearing a hot cup of tea and toast with strawberry jam – hooray! Her kindness made me teary. We exchanged shy smiles. She gestured vaguely downstairs and for the briefest moment her face assumed Vivian's po-faced expression to an absolute tee which made me smile. She inclined her head and I understood that I was destined for the chair. I sense that this gift for mime is not a lack of common language but perhaps an inability to speak at all.

With nothing to lose now, I was possessed by a sense of reckless abandon and felt in no hurry to comply with Vivian's wishes. Besides, it was Sunday. If I still had a job, this was my day off. I enjoyed my toast down to the last crumb, ran a bath and washed my hair. The day was already pleasantly warm. I dressed in a cotton frock and sandals and made my way down to Vivian's office.

Vivian is difficult to read at the best of times so it was impossible to discern whether she knew about last night. I am curious to know how much she and Mr Brooke actually communicate with each other. Clearly, just from the way they refer to each other, there is animosity between them. Do they even speak?

It is evident to me now that Vivian does nothing without careful consideration. She has the self-control to work toward an outcome unswayed by emotion, a quality that is admirable and intimidating in equal parts. I sat down opposite her, convinced this would be gloves off: full disclosure as to why I am here, what she wants from me and why Mr Brooke refuses to cooperate. Or I would simply be dismissed and probably never know. But it was neither. Amicable and charming, she reminded me it was Sunday and invited me to attend evening mass with herself and the guests. Although, she added apologetically, it was conducted entirely in French.

'Thank you, but I'm not a Roman Catholic, actually.' I was still not bold enough to admit I was raised as an atheist. I could see she was taken aback (was this a question Mr Hubert overlooked in the interview?) but forced a smile and made a quick recovery.

'My apologies; it's not a prerequisite of the job, obviously.' She adopted a sincere expression. 'But, of course, if you would ever like to join us you would be most welcome.'

I found myself nodding compliantly as if this were somehow likely. Honestly, this eager to please aspect of my personality disgusts me. I quite despise it in myself. It is nothing but a charming sort of cowardice.

'As I'm sure you have noticed, the upper part of the house is not yet refurbished,' continued Vivian. 'Normally I would have put you in a renovated guest room, but when Mrs Somerville was so keen to come I didn't have the heart to refuse her. When she leaves, you may have her room.'

Having seen signs that the place is running on a shoestring, it is understandable that she didn't have the heart to refuse Mrs Somerville's funds. I told her I was perfectly happy with my room. Her change of tack was most mysterious.

'Really?' We find each other equally perplexing. The English language is all we have in common. She's from a different class, a different world, and her only purpose in engaging me is as an instrument to get this thing she wants – if only I knew what it was!

'I really made no progress with Mr Brooke last week. I am not sure —'

'On the contrary – you're doing terribly well. But let's not worry about that now, this is your day off. Is there something you'd like to do? Monsieur Lapointe could drive you?'

In that moment I knew exactly what I wanted to do. 'I'd like to make a telephone call actually, just a local call.' I rushed back to my room and fetched the number. Vivian could barely conceal her curiosity as she instructed the operator to place the call. Moments later I was speaking to Alexander, my travelling companion from the train, and before very long we were flying down the hill in his dear little blue Austin Healey while he bombarded me with questions.

He wanted to know where the Brookes were from and how long they had been in Grasse. Was the villa a family estate, or had they bought it? Who were their people? Where did they get their money?

I felt so excited and relaxed to be out of that house, even though I barely know Alexander, and I found myself babbling like a fool. We drove straight to the coast, to the little town of Juan-les-Pins and a small hotel on the waterfront called Belles Rives. And all the while I gabbed on and on about Vivian, Jonathan, Menna, the Farleys, the strange Mr Geraldson and the shoe incident, culminating with the wine incident of last night. As before, Alexander was a splendid audience; he crowed with laughter at my mortification, was fascinated by Vivian and Mr Brooke, and adored the eccentricities of the guests.

We were given a table overlooking the sea, today blue and still as a lake. Without consulting me, Alexander ordered for us both and the waiter returned shortly with two tall champagne glasses filled with a dusky pink liquid that I was informed was a Bellini. It smelled like sunshine and tasted really quite pleasant.

'I'm perplexed that you haven't asked more questions of them,' he said. 'Is it just your middle-class manners?' He reached across the table and patted my hand. 'Do you think it's vulgar, dear?'

I laughed. 'Probably. Yes, I do think it's vulgar to ask personal questions, now you mention it. You obviously don't share that view?'

'Of course I do. However, gossip and mischief-making are a kind of drug for me,' he replied delicately, easing a Black Russian out of its pack and lighting up with a slim gold lighter. 'So I'm forced to be provocative.'

'I don't suppose you like being cross-examined, though.'

Relaxing back in his chair, he breathed smoke into the blue sky. 'On the contrary, I adore anyone taking the slightest interest — try me.'

'All right. How do you afford to live in the South of France, drive a luxury car and smoke expensive cigarettes?'

He laughed. 'Ah, straight to the heart of the matter – how clever of you. Good to know you do possess some questionable manners.' He beckoned the waiter over and spoke to him briefly before continuing, 'My parents pay me to live here. I may do whatever I please, provided I don't set foot in Britain.'

As I pondered this riddle, a bottle of white wine and a dozen oysters on ice, grey and glistening in their sinister shells, arrived at the table. Alexander must have sensed I was quietly mounting a protest. 'If you want to be a mermaid, start with the cuisine, I always say.' He picked up a shell, pried a rather odious looking creature loose and slid it into his mouth.

Although outwardly resistant, the Bellini had gone straight to my head and unleashed a dissolute recklessness within me. Without pausing to reconsider, I followed Alexander's example. Although the texture was rather suspect, it tasted like a morsel of ocean: bright and pure. I had a sip of the pale, cold wine and suddenly felt terribly grown up and sophisticated. If only the naysayers in the department could have seen me!

'Did you commit some sort of crime?' I asked half-jokingly.

'Many. I'm considered to be a dangerous criminal in Britain.'

'But not here?'

'Oh no, queers have been welcome here since the French Revolution,' he replied, quaffing his wine. '*Vive la révolution.*' Avoiding my eye, he gazed vaguely around the restaurant. 'Scott and Zelda Fitzgerald lived here, you know.' He looked at me then, not able to put the moment off any longer. 'For "welcome", read "tolerated".' There was an endearing uncertainty in his eyes.

As it turns out, the civil service has prepared me for more things in life than most people would imagine. We had a couple of chaps in the department who were almost certainly homosexual, although it was never acknowledged or discussed and neither were as obvious or flamboyant as Alexander. I knew them quite well; they were both very decent men and over the years I gained a sense of how difficult life is for men of their ilk.

'*Vive la révolution!*' I said, raising my glass. He touched his glass to mine and smiled a crinkly smile.

As the afternoon wore on, dish after dish arrived seemingly unbidden: fresh fish, salty butter-fried potatoes, peppered tomatoes with white cheese, followed by a slice of sweet lemon tart. All surprisingly edible. But finally my old enemy, the nasty black stuff, turned up. My attitude has always been that if you do not like something, then avoid it! But Alexander insisted this was the worst kind of English closed-mindedness toward all things foreign: culinary xenophobia. There was barely an inch of tar in the tiny cup and, doused liberally with sugar, it was almost bearable.

We left the hotel and motored around to nearby Antibes where we parked and wandered aimlessly around the quaint old town, through the narrow lanes now deep in late afternoon shadow. The town culminates in the rocky shoreline of the Mediterranean with views of Nice curved around a crescent bay and framed in the distance by the Italian Alps. It all seems so exotic to someone for whom the seaside has been the windswept beaches of the North Sea. No wonder people talk of the Mediterranean with an almost poetic reverence – there is a languor in the gentle swell of blue beckoning one over the horizon to North Africa.

Over the course of the afternoon, I tried to impress upon Alexander the predicament I was in, to convey the oppressive atmosphere of the house and why I felt so uncomfortable there. The way guests had to be tiptoed around as though they were live grenades. Vivian's ability to steer the conversation in any direction that suited her, which exacerbated the problem of Mr Brooke's adversarial and contrary behaviour. 'If I ask *him* a question, he simply ignores it and changes the subject.' It was a relief to share it with someone but Alexander remained unfazed, brushing off my concerns.

'It sounds overwhelmingly entertaining. I miss the theatre more than anything.' He sighed. 'It's all deeply Shakespearian: the blind brother held prisoner by his sister with a Machiavellian plan – perhaps there'll be a murder? If only I could take short-hand, I would take over when you leave.'

'How can I possibly leave?' I asked crossly, his trivialisation of my situation starting to get on my nerves.

'Come on now, don't be annoyed with me. Something will come up.'

'What is likely to come up?'

'A handsome Frenchman who will sweep you off your feet and sire a brood of little frogs for you to fuss over.'

'He'd better be quick,' I said. 'I'm almost over that particu-lar hill.'

He stopped and gazed into my face, his expression a carica-ture of sadness that was hard to take seriously. 'Do you know what we need?'

'What?'

'A drink!'

'Oh no, I've had far too much already; I'm becoming a lush,' I protested but soon we were back in the car heading around the bay. He pulled into a driveway where he parked with a dozen other motor cars in front of an imposing cream-coloured man-sion. The front door was opened by a man Alexander introduced as Robertson, who led us down the hallway toward the hum of a party and sounds of a violin being played rather savagely.

'Where are we? I'm not dressed for an occasion. I thought we were just calling on a friend,' I whispered.

'It's not an occasion, just a never-ending knees up.' He ran his eyes appraisingly over my cotton frock. 'You look fetchingly wholesome, like Dorothy minus the red shoes which would, in any case, be unbearably twee.'

Robertson rapped at the door. The violin stopped with a screech and the door was flung open to reveal a large, high-ceilinged room. Dizzying light reflected off a swimming pool beyond which were views to the sea. Several dozen people sat around on white settees and cushions; some men, some women, and a few seemingly undecided.

Alexander was greeted enthusiastically with a robust kiss on the mouth by our host, Freddy, an impish American dressed in tight, gold brocade matador trousers with a red cape flung across his bare chest – although there were no other indications this was a costume party. He had a violin in one hand, which he now mercifully put aside. Alexander introduced us but Freddy ignored my extended hand and proceeded to zealously kiss my cheeks. Once would have been awkward enough but three times was simply absurd. The French are terribly into kissing everyone they meet and quite undiscerning. Some British expats seem to have adopted this affectation as well. I don't care for it at all. The feel of a stranger's lips on my blushing cheeks makes me shudder.

'Look who's here, darlings! Now the party starts!' Freddy shrilled to no one in particular as he darted off to get us drinks and put a jazz record on the turntable. Alexander seemed positively subdued by comparison.

Two androgynous-looking women were entangled on the settee, joined at the lips. Both wore funereal black, making it difficult to see where one ended and the other began. A couple of men, who may have been wearing a little tastefully applied make-up, got up and danced together. A few people reclined on large cushions around a giant hookah pipe which was most likely responsible for the strange, sweet odour of burned apples that filled the room. I made an effort to be open-minded and resisted the desire to stare at people but it was hard to know where to rest one's gaze. On the surface, these people might have seemed troubled but my nose detected something quite joyous about this gathering. A distinct lack of the friction so evident at the villa.

When Freddy returned with two glasses of champagne, Alexander asked him, 'Is it indiscreet to enquire into the whereabouts of the *owner* of that —' he paused to select a suitably withering description – 'get up?'

Freddy took this as an invitation to kick up his heels and prance about, flourishing his cape at an imaginary bull. Tellingly, no one in the room bothered to turn and watch this embarrassing spectacle.

'In other words, is your toreador still on the premises?' Alexander insisted.

Freddy stopped his antics to point out, 'He's not a toreador – what do you take me for? He's a *mata*dor.'

'I realise I don't know the difference,' said Alexander.

'The toreador enrages the bull, the matador actually kills it,' I told him. 'It's more prestigious as it requires more skill.'

'Thank God,' said Freddy. 'You've finally befriended an intelligent woman.'

Not averse to the occasional compliment, I began to warm to

Freddy as a result of this one. I had already begun to develop a sense of compassion for him and the state he was in. Frantic for attention, his every pore exuded a reckless desperation.

An elegant, well-to-do looking couple drifted over to talk to Alexander and he introduced them as Topsy and Sebastian. They seemed relatively normal and were dressed in what I am coming to recognise as the casual Riviera style: shapeless linens inspired by peasants or shepherds. Both spoke with aristocratic drawls that reeked of old money and boredom but they seemed personable and welcoming.

Topsy looked me over thoroughly. 'I haven't seen you at Freddy's before.'

'No, I've only just arrived in France; Alexander brought me along.'

'You're very privileged,' Sebastian said. 'Freddy's notoriously selective – it took us ages to break in here, didn't it, Tops?'

'He calls these his Pansy Parties,' said Topsy. 'We adore them, you meet all the most fascinating people on the Côte d'Azur here. Sebastian's writing a novel, so he's always on the lookout for characters to put in it.'

'Oh, I thought novelists made up their characters.' I regretted this comment immediately as Topsy gave a derisive snort. 'And what do you do with yourself, Topsy?' I asked quickly.

'I watch him write.' She slipped her arm through his and they laughed at some private joke.

'If only that were true,' he said. 'She's a great distraction.'

'We also have several dreadfully naughty offspring who take over when I'm not available to distract him,' she said. She asked where I was living and I explained briefly, but at the mention of Villa Rousseau, Sebastian's ears pricked up.

'Ahhh, Hammond Brooke.' He said something in French which sounded like *le-ne*. For a moment I was perplexed, then the words and tune of a nursery rhyme we had sung along with the gramophone in Mrs Barker's class flooded back: 'Something, Something, *une bouche* and *le nez*.'

I stared at him uncomprehendingly. 'The nose?'

'*Oui*,' he replied. '*Le parfumeur*.'

'You don't know him? He's terribly famous. I thought he was dead,' said Topsy.

'Well, actually, he's blind,' I said.

'Blind?' asked Sebastian, taken aback. 'From the war?'

'I'm really not sure.' I had already said too much. Was I bound by secrecy outside the house as well? A perfumer? Why hadn't anyone told me? It's nothing to be ashamed of as far as I know.

'You must remember his most famous perfume, *Aurélie*?' said Topsy.

While I am no expert in the topic of scent, I did indeed remember this particular one. Who could forget it?

'Blind. How interesting,' said Sebastian. 'My family had a connection with the Brooke family back in England.' He stared into the distance, frowning with concentration. 'Our mothers knew each other. I remember going to see her once as a child, she was French – the mother – quite exotic —'

'Oh, darling, don't bore her with all that family nonsense. Have you been up to Monte Carlo yet, Iris?' asked Topsy.

Of course I hadn't, and assured her that I was far from bored, interested in anything they might know. But Sebastian had by now lost interest in the topic. He muddled about lighting his pipe, huffing and puffing to get the beastly thing going while

Topsy regaled me with tales of their gambling escapades, insisting I must join them next time. I told her I didn't have anything like the sort of money needed to gamble – let alone the expertise.

'I wouldn't worry about that,' she said. 'Alexander is determined to fritter away his parents' entire fortune. He's always looking for new ways to waste it.'

'What will he do when the money runs out?' I asked, dismayed by the irrationality of this scheme.

'Kill himself, I shouldn't wonder,' said Topsy airily, lighting up a cigarette, just to add to the fug. Even taking into account that she was a little tight, I began to dislike her. I don't approve of people being flippant about such things. I may not have known Alexander long but I'm already quite fond of him. Despite his gregariousness, I recognise something of myself in him. We both give off an air of being self-contained but are, in fact, more than a little lost.

Sebastian caught the look on my face and added quickly, 'She's joking, of course. I think Al feels that if they couldn't pay him to stay away he would be free to go back to England.'

'Don't they give him a limited allowance?' I asked.

'Supposedly, but he's terribly clever at squeezing more out of them,' said Topsy.

'That makes no sense at all,' I said. 'He doesn't have to take his parents' money.'

'Of course I do,' said Alexander, joining us. 'My only ambition in life is to see them destitute. Then I will be quite happy, my life's work complete.'

'And you would throw yourself off the Cape with bricks in your pockets,' added Topsy, seemingly determined to encourage this path of action. 'To compound their misery.'

'I'm not brave enough to throw myself off or under anything,' said Alexander. 'Perhaps I'd drink a bottle of gin and then swim toward Africa until I wearied and drifted off into a deep sleep.'

'What nonsense!' I said but he laughed and helped himself to another glass of champagne and savoury delicacies brought around by an older woman wearing a deep tan and a voluminous Oriental silk robe. 'Why not do something clever?' I suggested. 'So people admire you and your parents realise how mistaken they've been in exiling you.'

All three gazed at me with indulgent smiles. Feeling patronised and foolish, I announced I was going to look at the view (in what I hope was a haughty tone) and walked stiffly across the room and out onto the patio. A man was swimming lazy laps of the pool, dark-skinned and compact; the water sloughed off his muscular back as his arms and torso moved in perfect accord. This, I assumed, was the matador.

I stood at the railing and looked out over the sea, a gentle sway of violet silk in the fading light, and puzzled over the information that had serendipitously come my way. Mr Brooke a perfumer. It explained so much – the peculiar smell in his house for a start.

Somewhere tucked away in a box at Linnet Lane is the long-empty bottle that I never had the heart to throw away. I remember that summer so well. It was a year or two after the war when this strange foreign word began to tumble off British women's lips in a fully-ripened French accent – with mixed results. It seemed the whole of London was obsessed by this mysterious fragrance and every woman determined to have a bottle of *Aurélie*. I had yearned for one myself and put money aside until I could afford it.

While I have a special interest in all things olfactory, it's more related to actual smells as opposed to artificial scent. Nevertheless, I became fascinated by the enigma that surrounded this particular fragrance that reputedly offered a different experience to every wearer. Although I don't ever recall a perfume being so avidly discussed before, the qualities of *Aurélie* were debated during tea breaks. No one could agree on the truth of the fragrance; pragmatists became poetic in an effort to find an interpretation. I heard it variously described as ethereal, perhaps like clouds or mist. Others detected an oceanic saltiness or a pungent earthiness. Everyone seemed to believe it contained their favourite flower: gardenia, rose, lavender, jasmine, violet. But it was evident to me that focusing on the floral aspect was to oversimplify a complex alchemy as elusive as falling in love.

Perhaps I was drawn by the mystique of the fragrance but that time stands out in my memory as one when I felt at my most confident and self-assured. I had a sense of being fully in the world. And I wasn't the only one. *Aurélie* was like a narcotic; women couldn't get enough of it. According to hearsay, it worked its magic indiscriminately from the budding of adolescence to the full bloom of maturity. It was a rite of passage, an aphrodisiac, a panacea. It was said to ignite new love and rekindle old. Soon it was difficult to differentiate the myth from the reality, it was self-fulfilling. But within a couple of years *Aurélie* was in short supply. Women queued outside department stores with stock. And then, as mysteriously as it arrived, it disappeared.

I remember noticing that imitations had sprung up but these were travesties of the original. One even attempted to cash in with an anglicised version, '*Oralee*: French perfume for the English Lady'. Nothing came close to the effect *Aurélie* had on the average

British woman who, for a short time in her life, felt sanctified, her quintessential self. All of these pretenders to the throne quickly sank back into obscurity and eventually we forgot all about *Aurélie* – apart from a lingering whiff in the empty bottle.

Now, having given thought to the implications of my new-found knowledge about Hammond Brooke, I felt even more intimidated by the task ahead but curious too. I should have liked to go home then as I was tired and wanted to think, but Alexander was in no state to take me and so I waited for him to sober up. The rest of the evening passed in a kind of blur.

Topsy got it into her silly head that I should leave the Brooke household and become her *au pair*. I gathered that 'servant troubles' were a constant irritation for Topsy and Sebastian but neither seemed to have any insight into the possibility that they contributed to the problem. The woman in the Oriental gown was a soothsayer or perhaps a fortune teller – I'm not sure of the difference; anyhow, she badgered me about the time and date of my birth and made some obtuse predictions that could have equally applied to anyone in the room but I was too tired to really take it in.

Finally Freddy, now in the grip of a feverish excitement, picked up the violin and I was not alone in deeming it time to leave – there was a crush to get through the door. Unfortunately, Alexander was by then in an even worse state and I refused his slurred offer to drive me home. He packed me into a taxi, handing the driver such a large sum of money that the man took off at breakneck speed either to demonstrate willingness or to escape before being asked for change. The fellow kept up the pace and I had to cling to the hand strap to avoid being thrown around on the tight bends up the hills.

It was a relief to reach my dismal little room at midnight. On the desk was a bowl of strawberries and an envelope bearing my name scrawled so untidily that it could have been written by a blind man. The note inside read, *'Forgive me – HB'*. It was written in an unrepentant scrawl that left a splatter of ink across the page. I don't know about forgiving him. I am almost certain that he is only saying it because he wants something, not because he cares that he upset me. But he tends to choose his words carefully. No one wants to be thought unforgiving. Perhaps the role of nanny for the rather tiresome Topsy could have a certain appeal – if only because she seems a little simple-minded, as opposed to Mr Brooke, who is endlessly shrewd.

Chapter Five

I went to the sunroom for breakfast early this morning, hoping to avoid any guests, but Mr Geraldson was already seated at the table drinking his coffee, eating bread with ham and smoking while he read *Le Figaro*. As I sat down, he glanced up briefly and murmured a cursory greeting. Without taking his eyes off the page, he asked, 'And how is your work progressing, Miss Turner?'

I wasn't even aware he knew my name and my mind began working furiously to make sense of his question. What did he know? Was this was a trap of his own invention? Or a test contrived by Vivian? I can't quite fathom his role here and what his interest might be. It is unnerving that so many people appear to be watching me.

'I'm not sure what you mean.'

'You know perfectly well what I'm talking about.'

'Oh, you mean my work for Miss Brooke?' I busied myself with breakfast in the hope that would be the end of it.

He rose from his chair, folded his newspaper and tossed it

onto the table. 'Are you really as innocent as you appear, I wonder?' He gave me a calculating look, stubbed his cigarette on his plate and left the room without another word. Insufferable man.

All the way to the cottage I was debating whether to reveal to Mr Brooke what I had learned about him. Perhaps this was my opportunity to bring things out in the open and make some real progress? In the end it seemed better to keep quiet for the moment in the hope of more information drifting in my direction.

He sat out on his terrace. I called out a greeting, not wanting to startle him, and observed with some satisfaction that my tone sounded more businesslike; an improvement on my earlier obsequiousness.

'So, you're back,' he said, but then soured the moment by adding, 'Hip hooray.'

'I know who you are,' I blurted, perhaps as a result of his barb.

'I'm delighted one of us does. Where are you getting your information?'

'I went to a party and met some English people —' I began, sitting down beside him.

'Idle gossip, in other words. And what did you tell them?'

'Simply that I worked for Miss Brooke.'

'And does your new information change anything?'

'Well, I'm trying to understand —'

He turned his face to me, his temper barely under control. 'If you used a modicum of intelligence, and clearly you possess some, what you would "understand" is – as previously stated –

I did not hire you. Nor do I actually want you here. I am under duress. So hearing that you are now out and about twittering to your new chums is not what I want to hear.'

Anything I said now would only further inflame him, so I was silent. After a moment he redirected his furious gaze toward the garden. His face softened. Perhaps he could make out some shapes and he could no doubt smell the creamy jonquils, ruby tulips and irises in royal purple that sprung from patches of lily-of-the-valley and the fragrance of jasmine that filled the air. But he could not see the glorious blaze of colour in the bright morning sun. I knew he could hear the birds calling, the whispering of the bees and creak of cicadas. But I wondered how it felt to have all this beauty at your feet and see nothing but shadows.

'Some more hyacinths have bloomed,' I said. 'A very pretty mauve colour.'

He was silent for a moment and it seemed he was still annoyed, then he asked, 'Could you cut one for me? There are secateurs on the windowsill.'

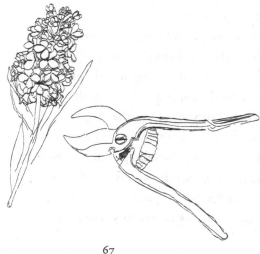

I fetched the freshly sharpened secateurs out of their leather pouch, cut a hyacinth and placed it in his palm. There was a moment when our hands brushed and I quickly pulled away. He must have sensed something as he looked amused. He held the hyacinth at chest height, took a deep breath and another and then, like an angry child, hurled the flower away from him. We fell back into silence.

'I need you to be patient,' he said finally.

I was taken aback by the sincerity in his voice. 'Of course, but it would help me if I knew what exactly Miss Brooke wanted.'

He gave an extravagant sigh. 'All right. I'm prepared to offer some small compromise to Vivian's wishes, provided you don't ask questions or talk about things that are simply none of your business.'

He really can be frightfully rude, but I nevertheless agreed.

So, we got through that. He then asked me to fetch a parcel from the dining table inside, which I did. It was a small package that had been posted from London some weeks before. I thought he would want me to unwrap it but he held out his hand impatiently.

He slowly undid the string, peeled back the thick brown paper, all the time inhaling evenly as though he were attempting to chart the actual journey of the parcel; inhaling the particles released by the paper as it was cut, the twine freed from its roll, the hands that wrapped it, the post box, sorting room, mailbag and finally the scent of his own kitchen table. He caressed the book it contained, weighing it in his hands with evident satisfaction. He opened it and lifted it to his face, breathing in the essence of the printed page.

Fascinating as it was to witness, he seemed to derive no

pleasure from the experience but abruptly handed it to me and asked if I would read to him. And so it was that the rest of the morning was spent reading aloud – not one of the great works of literature one might have imagined – but Ian Fleming's latest outpouring entitled *Moonraker*.

I really can't complain; it was pleasant sitting in the sun, reading aloud, and it felt as though I were doing something useful for a change. Toward lunchtime, he suddenly got up and went inside. Returning a few minutes later, he settled himself down with evident satisfaction. 'I've told them to bring your lunch down here. So you won't have to dine with those insufferable fools today. Continue.'

I was momentarily stunned by his assumption but had little choice but to push on. Half an hour later, Menna arrived with a tray that held two bowls of soup and a baguette, which she placed on the garden table, and laid two places carefully with cutlery and napkins.

Stretching and yawning, Mr Brooke got up and wandered over to the table. Menna's eyes met mine for a second and I had a sense of her concern for me – which was very touching. Mr Brooke turned his head, as though hearing something in the silence itself. He thanked her briskly as he pulled out his chair, scraping it across the gravel, but she was already on her way back to the villa.

We sat opposite one another at the small circular table, our knees almost touching. He held his bowl at chin height for better accuracy. 'You were going to tell me about your mother,' he said.

'Oh, I don't know why you'd be interested in my family.'

'In case you haven't noticed, I lead the dullest of lives. You implied there was some mystery – that intrigued me.'

Perhaps he was bored; I doubt he was genuinely interested, but, in any case, I embarked on the story which I will record here for posterity.

My mother ran away right after the war. She left a note bidding us farewell, the tone of which was unapologetic. In summary, the war years had been the best of her life. She had not wanted to return home. She owed it to my father to give it a shot but her heart was elsewhere and she was following it. She had gone and would not return.

Strangely, Father could be calm and rational when faced with a letter from his wife saying she had left forever. Written in her neat, familiar hand, he could read it and quietly digest its contents and implications in his own time. However, had the door knocker clacked or the telephone trilled during this digestion process, it would be a different story. He was sensitive to the slightest sound and, once agitated, crossed into a dark void where he flailed around with no sense of the pain he inflicted or the casualties.

Initially I was more curious than distressed about the note. Mother had, after all, been away for most of the war years. Her visits home on leave had been fleeting and distracted, often interrupted by mysterious disappearances, apparently visiting friends. Over that period, she had become a different person; younger, livelier and less responsible – more like a sister. She even went so far as to ask me to call her Clare rather than Mother at one point. In retrospect that was more significant than I gave it credit for at the time.

Clare was nineteen years old when she met my father, Henry, sometime during 1920 at Murray's Night Club in Beak Street.

Light on his feet, he was busy making up for those years lost to the war by working his way through the clubs that were springing up all over London at that time.

Clare had been academic at school, topping her class in mathematics. She had wanted to go on to university but her parents thought it a waste. Unlike me, who toddled off to Secretarial School without a murmur of protest, she was more spirited and rebelled by running away to London. To a young woman newly arrived from the north, Henry must have seemed brave and worldly. His scarred jowl added an heroic element to his even, handsome features. Two months later they were married. I came into the world the same year and Alan arrived a year later.

Clare was barely forty when war broke out and she leapt at the chance to tear off her apron and join the army. She trained as a radar operator. Older than many of the other female recruits, she showed a rare talent for the work, perhaps because of her aptitude for mathematics. After training, she was sent to Suffolk to the radar station at Bawdsey Manor. She loved having valuable work and the respect of colleagues, something she had never had the chance to experience. It was as though she had been waiting her whole life for this opportunity to shine. A year later she was commissioned as a Second Lieutenant and came home on leave proudly sporting one pip on her shoulder. And so the die was cast.

By the time she left us for good, I was twenty-five years old. Father, perhaps not trusting himself to deal with the situation rationally, instructed me to find out her whereabouts and talk some sense into her. I telephoned my grandparents, who lived in Ormskirk, and extracted from my nan that they had seen Clare briefly and that she had gone back to Suffolk. So on the Saturday I took the train to Suffolk and the tiny hamlet of Bawdsey. Initially Clare had lived in the women's quarters within the manor but once commissioned she was moved into a more comfortable billet with a local family, Mr and Mrs Curtis and their two sons. They lived close enough to the manor that she could ride her bicycle to work.

I found the address easily enough; I had often written to her there. Mrs Curtis was at home. Her face puffy and mottled, she nodded glumly as I explained the situation and then kindly invited me in. The house smelled damp with sorrow and regret. We sat in the kitchen watching her two boys play football in the garden. Beyond lay peaceful green fields and woodlands that stretched into the distance. Mrs Curtis wept, trembling uncontrollably as she made tea and in the end I helped her to a chair and made the tea myself. Mr Curtis, she explained, had left yesterday and was now living in sin with my mother in nearby Felixstowe. I knew already that Mr Curtis had lost an arm fighting in France in 1942 and had been seconded as a school teacher in the local school for the remainder of the war. The trouble didn't start right away, she explained, but she could see it brewing. 'George is a gentle man; quiet. He never wanted to go to the war and, when he came back, he just couldn't accept his injury.'

'She – your mother – was on duty all hours so we hardly saw her. She just slept here. Sometimes we didn't see her for days but then she'd have a twenty-four-hour leave and sleep half the day or sit in the garden drying her hair in the sun or whatever.' Mrs Curtis dissolved into tears. 'He'd be his normal grumpy self then she'd walk in the room and he'd light up and suddenly turn into what you might call a sparkling conversationalist. Showing off, he was. Flirting. I came home one afternoon and they were sat on the settee, pretending to have a conversation but I just *knew* that two minutes earlier they'd been all over each other.'

'Did you talk to him about it?' I asked.

'I was too afraid. I didn't want to bring it out in the open. First off, I wanted to get her reallocated but then I realised I wouldn't be able to keep an eye on him, and, worse, the whole village would find out about it. So I waited for it to wear itself out.' She dabbed her eyes with her handkerchief. 'That was my first thought when the war ended. It took six weeks before she was demobbed and I was finally rid of her.' She burst into a fresh bout of crying. 'He was like a ghost when she'd gone. I thought he'd get over it. Now, only a week later, this! He didn't give us a second thought, me and the boys.'

My mother had gone and stolen the father of two small boys and wrecked this poor woman's life but all I could think about was what on earth to tell my father.

Evidently the diminished, ghostly George Curtis had been waiting for a message. When his marching orders arrived from Clare, he came to life, took the stairs two at a time, packed his bag and told Mrs Curtis the brutal truth – he was head over heels in love.

'As I said, he's a kind man – or was,' said Mrs Curtis sadly. 'But it was like a fever in him. I suppose, he never thought, you know, with him damaged goods and all . . .'

She saw me to the door and gave me the name of the guest-house where Clare and George were staying in Felixstowe. As I stepped outside into the freezing wind blowing off the North Sea, she asked, 'Are you going to see them? Would you mind taking his warm jacket?' She gazed up into the leaden sky. 'I think this weather's going to take a turn for the worse.'

Clare and George, now masquerading as Mr and Mrs George Curtis, were holed up in a greasy, rundown guesthouse two streets back from the seaside. At my knock, there was a palpable silence, then Clare called out, 'Who is it?' On identifying myself there was another long silence, underpinned by hushed murmurings. She opened the door a crack, enough to reveal that she was wearing the clichéd night attire of a 1940s screen siren. A fruity animal heat seeped out of the room. Behind her I could see an unmade bed, grey tangled sheets.

'Hello, love,' she said with a quick nervous smile, as though she hoped to avoid this conversation. I handed her George's warm jacket and suggested we meet in the pub across the road. She nodded and quickly closed the door.

In the pub I nursed a lemonade and fumed with angry resentment for a good twenty minutes before she came hurrying through the door hugging her coat to her. She ordered a shandy and brought it to the table. Fresh from her bath, her hair was in a topknot, tiny curls clinging damply to her neck, giving the treacherous home-wrecker a sweet childlike vulnerability. She sat down and covered my hand with hers. The spiteful child in me was tempted to snatch my hand away but something stopped me. There was sorrowful apology in her eyes but no disguising the radiance that illuminated her every cell. I realised with a thump of my heart that I had never seen my mother truly happy.

The heaviness that had weighed on me from the moment I read her note lifted. In that moment I detached from her and we became separate beings. The final protective skin of childhood was sloughed away. I saw my mother through adult eyes as an individual who, despite her obligations, could do what she damn well pleased with her life. I realised that despite the pain she had caused, what she had done was terrifyingly courageous. She had grasped the chance of happiness with both hands, and George had done the same – though only with the one hand, obviously.

I delivered the message from my father – which was about as romantic as a bill of sale – and although she was remorseful, Clare was resolute. She asked if I would like to meet George, and despite the hesitancy of my agreement, she darted out the door with an energy I hadn't seen before. A moment later she returned with a large shambling man, the empty left sleeve of his jacket tucked neatly in his pocket. He wasn't a handsome hero, just an ordinary chap with a slow smile and kind eyes. In spite of everything, I liked him. As it happened, it was the last time I would ever meet him.

I caught the train home that evening and conveyed the basic information to my father and Alan – neither of whom asked me a single question about her situation. Father made his own interpretation. Like Mrs Curtis, he preferred to sit with the idea that this infatuation would wear itself out and Mother would eventually come home, whereupon life could resume as before. Waiting gave him no peace but we never spoke of it again.

As for Clare and George, they left Suffolk soon after and set up house near Dundee, where George had found a teaching post. Only a year later, on a sightseeing holiday on the west coast, George, perhaps hampered by his disability, failed to take a corner. Their car left the road and plunged down a bank into Loch nan Druimnean, where they both drowned.

Part of me believes that had she stuck to the original well-trodden path of her life, my mother would still be alive. But the fatalist in me wonders if this was the trajectory that life always had in store for her . . . in which case, at least she had that time of supreme happiness, something many people never have the chance to experience.

As for myself, I regret not having more time with her. I took it for granted she would always be there. As the years pass, I miss her more deeply and in different ways. I miss the possibilities for our adult relationship. I'm sure if he allowed himself to think about it, Alan would feel the same. On the odd occasion when we have a moment alone, there may be a wistful mention of her but we have learned the hard way to never let the conversation stray in that direction within earshot of Ruth. We have an unspoken understanding that Ruth's condemnation of our mother and her 'immoral' behaviour (cloaked in the guise of loyalty to Alan, but actually because Ruth is the self-appointed standard-bearer of suburban morality) leaves us both feeling emotionally flayed. We loved our mother.

Although I obviously told Mr Brooke a highly edited version of this story, I could see he was moved. Reaching across the table toward me, he asked for my hand. Slightly confused, I offered my hand as if to shake his. He took it and held my palm gently against his cheek. He held it for so long that my self-consciousness disappeared. I began to feel that I was in the hands of a practitioner and allowed him to absorb whatever it was he needed. I would be patient. I could feel the texture of his skin on my fingertips, the hardness of his cheekbone and it was as though we had made a connection that, even a few minutes ago, seemed impossible. We seemed to have so many misfires and misunderstandings but there was a sense of peace between us then. The incendiary smell that usually fills the air around him had dissipated and something more gentle and poignant emerged: loneliness, regret.

So, that was the highlight of my day but now I need to bathe and dress for dinner – such a tiresome business to have to endure every single night! I truly long for a simple supper and a warm little cat curled up in my lap.

Dinner was a splendid roast of beef with Yorkshire pudding and all the trimmings but my mind was elsewhere, and guests had to ask me several times to pass the gravy boat or the salt and pepper. Vivian looked at me curiously and I made a concerted effort to snap out of my dream state. It was not so much the incident with Mr Brooke as the hour this evening spent writing my mother's tragic story that has stayed with me.

Oddly, Mr Farley was at dinner without his dear little other, so Mrs Somerville assumed he was available for some light sparring. She blazed away at the wrong-headedness of British colonialists and then moved onto the French, who had lost control in Algeria – two arrogant, deluded colonial powers whose glory days were over. Despite Vivian's best efforts to divert her, she pushed on until Mr Farley, who had barely looked up from his supper, launched back at her. 'Madam, French imperialists cannot hold a candle to the British Empire when it comes to the management of their colonies. One cannot speak of them in the same breath.'

Mrs Somerville puffed up excitedly like a songbird about to warble but Mr Farley wasn't bridging any interruption. 'In the words of the great Cecil Rhodes, the British are the finest race in the world and the more of it we inhabit the better. No one ever said that about the French.'

'That we know of,' added Jonathan under his breath.

But Mr Farley wasn't finished. 'The French seem to overlook the fact that their colonies do not share their own high opinion of themselves – unlike British subjects who, far and wide, *recognise* us as a superior race. We give savages something to aspire to.'

While this absurd (and embarrassing!) debate raged, I found myself watching Mr Geraldson. Throughout the discussion he had maintained his usual detachment. However, when Mr Farley, determined to overrun Mrs Somerville, turned to his compatriot and asked, 'Don't you agree, Geraldson?' it was as though Geraldson were an actor as he stepped smoothly into the part, adding his concurrence. It dawned on me then that despite his upper-class pretensions and refined enunciation, Mr Geraldson is not British. There's something foreign about him. Not just that he eats bread with ham for breakfast; more a sense that he's playing the part of an English gentleman.

Once Mr Farley had established that he and Mr Geraldson were in accord, he gave a thin smile and excused himself. Lady Jessica was apparently feeling poorly and he needed to attend to her, which left Mrs Somerville looking rather deflated. I have to admire her: she's plucky taking him on and quite the progressive thinker.

The most extraordinary thing just happened. It was late when I finished the last entry this evening and, feeling peckish, decided to tiptoe down to the kitchen for something to placate my hunger pangs. The house was in darkness but a full moon threw slabs of cold light through the windows and I found my way easily down the winding service stair.

As I approached the kitchen via the scullery off the service hallway, I noted something unusual in the air – there was a dense, rich, earthy smell but with a tingling charge to it, like the aftermath of a thunderstorm. The door to the kitchen was closed and the room in darkness but through the glass inset I saw the most astonishing sight: the silhouette of a naked woman standing beside the kitchen table. Her breasts flashed white in the moonlight. She bent down, perhaps to slip off her panties as she then tossed an item across the room. I recognised her immediately by the fall of her hair. It was too dark to make out her expression. I wondered had she lost her mind? Should I fetch a blanket or just slip away? Crouching down, I changed the angle of my view and spotted a cigarette tip glowing red in the darkness, then flicked toward the sink. The silhouette of a man moved toward the woman and she momentarily disappeared in his shadow. Then a flare of moonlight illuminated her cheek as he lifted her onto the table and she pulled him into an embrace, her legs wrapping around his waist. Compelling as the scene was, I had now crossed the fine line between curiosity and voyeurism, so slipped back up the stairs to my room. What a to-do!

Chapter Six

On reflection, I'm thoroughly annoyed about the kitchen incident last night. Vivian has a perfectly good bedroom in which to conduct her torrid affairs. It is outrageous that an innocent party seeking a late-night snack is subjected to the spectacle of her employer stark naked – let alone in congress with a strange man. I have no idea if this is normal behaviour for Vivian or something inspired by the full moon – perhaps a rite of spring? How on earth will I face her today having seen her in the altogether? I do hope she retrieved her knickers off the kitchen floor. She's normally so fastidious. And who is the lover? Really none of my business, but it's difficult not to be insanely curious.

I feel a little strange about venturing down to the cottage this morning. When Mr Brooke took my hand yesterday I felt as though there was some sort of breakthrough of understanding between us. But now I'm not so certain. Perhaps I was caught up in the strange intimacy of the moment and misunderstood the situation? I'm worried the whole business about him pushing to hear my mother's story was to somehow manipulate me, to make me more vulnerable to him. I just don't know him well enough to decide.

Things have been calm and pleasant in the house this week, mainly due to a festive atmosphere created by the royal wedding. Mr Brooke has taken no interest apart from expressing his reservations as to how an American actress could fit into the situation, which according to him, was already complicated. He did reveal in passing that he had met Prince Rainier on several occasions as well as Princess Charlotte, whose personal fragrances were created by his grandfather, Monsieur Rousseau.

Mrs Somerville hired a driver to take herself and Lady Jessica to Monte Carlo (despite Mr Farley's disapproval) to join the throngs waiting to see Princess Grace leave the cathedral. From their account it was something of a crush with only distant glimpses of the royal couple. They probably saw less than the rest of us who watched a blow-by-blow account on the television set Vivian has recently installed in a small, rather inhospitable sitting room. Even in slightly fuzzy black-and-white, Princess Grace radiated beauty and goodness. I do so hope she will be happy.

On the subject of beauty and goodness, I received a splendidly long letter from Colleen detailing all the latest gossip in the department with a sweet postscript noting how proud she is of her friend in France. I suspect my letters to her may have overstated the good aspects and understated the difficulties of my situation.

My relationship with Mr Brooke has definitely improved and he is far more cordial. We finished *Moonraker* which was quite a satisfactory experience for both of us and have been able to discuss things more amicably. While nothing specific has been discussed about exactly what Vivian wants me to achieve, it's fairly clear that she has plans for me to document something relating to the perfume business which, from what I can gather, has long since closed down. Despite Jonathan's allusion to 'hocus-pocus', it seems unlikely it would have anything to do with formulas or compositions since surely these would be recorded at the time of creation? So that makes no sense.

Anyhow, we have actually started on some work, which is heartening. We spent quite some time sorting through a mish-mash of documents he wanted categorised and filed. In the main these were invoices and bills of lading relating to raw materials: essences and oils. There were hundreds of telegrams he wanted filed in date order too. These were mostly perfume orders from all over the world, but particularly the Middle East; dozens from Libya and Kuwait. It was a painful and protracted case of the inept leading the blind: me stumbling through unpronounce-able names of suppliers and merchandise and him (increasingly irritable) trying to guess at and correct my mistakes. The busi-ness was run from a factory nearby in Grasse, so it seems odd that these are even in his possession. Also strange is that the paperwork has been thrown higgledy-piggledy into cartons as though ransacked from its original filing system.

Late in the afternoons, when he has tired of the work, we have tea and play chess in a nice companionable way – although he does like to win. He has a purpose-made board with the black squares raised slightly above the white. The chess pieces have a tiny spike to hold them in place. I had often played chess with my father so am quite adept at allowing my opponent to win by a whisker when appropriate.

Despite his deep relationship with scents, Mr Brooke never so much as alludes to his own sense of smell, which must be highly refined and sensitive. He often comments on sounds he hears – the rain on the roof, an afternoon breeze riffling leaves, the peep of swallows as they dart about the eaves. Sounds but never smells. It's as though he's taken down his shingle and shut up shop. Today, over the chessboard, he asked about my earlier comment about smelling frustration. He asked how, specifically, I could smell such a thing.

'I don't fully understand it,' I admitted. 'I suppose it's an amalgam of smells that tap into a memory, or perhaps an association with an emotion or state of being. It's not an exact science. I do get it wrong occasionally.'

'Smell is essentially vibration,' he said. 'Vibration and memory. You were right. I am deeply frustrated by the fact that, could I still work, the depth and breadth of my emotional experience now would enhance my art above anything I have ever achieved. Perhaps there is nothing left to achieve but there is nothing else in the world I want to do. Apart from —' He stopped himself then.

'Yes?'

'Apart from move aside. When the time is right. Let things take their natural course.'

'Perhaps I can help,' I said without having a clue as to what he meant.

He thought about this for some time and finally said, 'Perhaps you can indeed.'

———

Vivian approached me in the drawing room this evening, emitting her usual high-frequency anxiety signals, and I was able to assure her in good conscience that work was well underway. Immaculately groomed as ever, she is so unlike the creature I witnessed in the kitchen the other night it has been impossible to connect the two – did I dream it?

Dinners this week have been a quiet affair. The Farleys have had meals sent to their room. Actually, I haven't seen Lady Jessica for the past few days. I do know she was poorly as they had the doctor up yesterday, but the weather has been so beautiful it seems peculiar that she hasn't at least come out to take in the afternoon sun on the patio. I feel sorry for her being stuck in that room with the awful Mr Farley.

I have also begun to feel sorry for the abrasive Mrs Somerville. She is obviously here because she's lonely but she lacks the requisite social skills for this kind of environment. As does Mr Geraldson; he eats his dinner in that particular way he has and barely acknowledges the other guests. I am a little curious to know what he does with himself during the day. He drives off in his car every morning and returns in the afternoon just in time to prepare for dinner. It seems as though he's here for business rather than leisure, given he treats the place like a boarding house – an expensive one at that. Interestingly, Mr Farley seems to share my curiosity. Finally we have something in common. Considering he holds his own privacy so dear, I have heard him ask both Jonathan and Vivian about Geraldson. Like Mr Brooke, Farley is also interested in the man's war service. Even ten years on, it seems important for men to know this information as a way of placing someone – knowing where they fought and, perhaps in this case, on which side. Both Vivian and Jonathan claimed no knowledge about Geraldson, which I know is patently untrue.

Although he can be irksome, Jonathan is adept at light conversation and puts in an effort to make the evenings convivial. He always compliments me on my clothes, which are really nothing much, and makes a point of remarking on my healthy complexion – often using exactly the same adjectives as the evening before. It seems that charm is a sort of currency for him and little wonder it's got him into trouble with women. He is forever fobbing Vivian off when she tries to coax him into accepting trunk calls from various ex-wives and offspring demanding his attention. His usual excuse is that he is terribly busy and will call them later – which I am quite sure he never does.

I had been looking forward to a quiet lunch with Alexander today – a welcome opportunity to dissect everything. But as soon as I got into his car I sensed he was in a odd mood and it dawned on me that although we have quickly become chums, we don't know each other all that well. After a lack of response to my solicitous overtures, we drove for twenty minutes in silence. He then informed me (a little tersely) that we were invited to lunch with Topsy and Sebastian. They were apparently 'desperate' to see me, having been enchanted by my 'unaffected' ways – whatever that is supposed to mean. At that point, adding numbers to our little party seemed a good idea.

Topsy and Sebastian live in a sumptuous house high in the hills above Cannes with views up and down the coastline. House is too modest a word – it's really a mansion with a veritable firmament of crystal chandeliers and acres of marble floors occasionally interrupted by staircases sweeping up to other levels of unimaginable luxury. A miasma of boredom (an unpleasant dusty smell like a forgotten sack of flour) hung in the air.

Alexander and I were ushered in by a pompous uniformed butler and taken through a grand dining room into a sitting room of more modest proportions. We were offered drinks. I requested tea and Alexander champagne which were duly delivered by a maid. Sebastian wandered in, drink in hand, and the two men went through the rigmarole of lighting cigarettes (fortunately the pipe seems to have lost favour!) as they exchanged desultory pleasantries. I was almost relieved when Topsy gusted into the room in a flurry of kissing and small talk. 'Isn't Freddy coming?' she asked Alexander.

'He's gone to Madrid,' he replied. 'Chasing his little toreador.'

'Matador,' I corrected.

'Quite.' Alexander had been glum before but having admitted the source of his melancholy he now sunk into deeper gloom.

'Ohhh dear, how disappointing,' Topsy cooed. 'We were so looking forward to hosting him here. Weren't we, Seb?'

Sebastian switched on his noncommittal smile that makes him look a little daft. I asked him how his novel was going and he said not well. Too many interruptions. Did that include us, I wonder? The butler returned to announce that lunch was served and threw open the doors to a small dining room where the table was beautifully laid for six people.

'Will your children be joining us?' I asked as we took our seats.

Sebastian and Topsy both crowed with laughter at the idea. 'What an unbearable thought!' she said. She flapped her bejewelled fingers in the vague direction of upstairs. 'They have their own little fiefdom where Nanny is entirely in command. No,

Sebastian's cousin, William Beaumont, will be joining us. He had some meeting or other so I said we would go on without him.'

The butler served up an oily fishy soup that impressed everyone but me. The talk turned to social arrangements and gossip about people I didn't know which allowed me to drift off and think of other things. Just as the main course was being served, the door opened and a quietly handsome fellow in his forties was shown in by the maid.

'Iris, William. William, Iris,' said Topsy. He nodded in my direction and sat down next to Topsy, who gave his shoulders a vigorous brush as though he were a dusty antique needing cleaning up for a potential customer. It occurred to me that since he wore no wedding band perhaps I was the intended customer? 'Iris is a chum of Freddy's,' said Topsy.

'Truly, I barely know Freddy,' I said. William seemed not particularly interested in any case.

'I spoke to my mother about Hammond Brooke,' said Sebastian. 'She was shocked, I must say – about him being blind.' My heart sank at the thought that my indiscretion had now crossed the channel.

'I was right, Mummy was friendly with his mother; her name was Camille,' he continued. 'She had apparently followed her father, Monsieur Rousseau, into the family perfume business. They had a factory up in Grasse. They were both respected "noses" but she died in a motor accident when Hammond was quite young. His father was English. He put the boy into board. Harrow, I believe.'

'What line of business was Hammond's father in?' asked Topsy.

'I think she said he was in the spice trade. In which case,

I expect he would have spent most of his time travelling abroad.'

'So where was Vivian?' I asked.

'Vivian?' repeated Sebastian.

'His sister.'

'There wasn't any mention of a sister. Vivian, you say?'

'It would be fascinating to meet Mr Brooke,' said Topsy. 'Do you think you could wrangle an introduction, Iris?'

It was difficult to explain what a preposterous idea this was so I didn't bother trying, but murmured I would give the matter some thought.

'Freddy is really such a nuisance making us uneven numbers,' said Topsy. 'I thought we could play a rubber or two of bridge after lunch. Do you play, Iris?'

'I have played. I may be a little rusty.'

'You four play. I'm not in the mood anyway,' said Alexander.

'Perfect. Seb and I can play against William and Iris – you two will make a great team.' She dealt us conspiratorial smiles, as though we were party to her unsubtle attempts at matchmaking that made us both squirm. I tried to avoid William's eye which wasn't difficult since he was playing the same game.

Alexander stretched out on the settee affecting a tragic pose while we played bridge, which was a bit of fun but I was glad when the afternoon came to an end. William is one of those people whose naturally sad expression is transformed by his smile. He seemed to go out of his way not to encourage my interest in any way which is probably a kindness.

As Alexander drove me back to the villa I asked, 'Surely they didn't acquire all that wealth through Sebastian's writing?'

'Lord, no! He encourages the idea of the tortured writer – probably because his life is relentlessly pleasant and easy. His writing is excruciating. If he ever asks you to read something, make an excuse. Feign illiteracy.'

'I doubt he'd want my opinion of his writing,' I said.

'You'd be surprised how low some people will stoop for a tiny glimmer of approbation. No, his family's in the whisky business. Hers are in gin. Or it could be the other way around. In any case, they're a distillery dynasty – slowly drowning in money.'

I wasn't sure whether to broach the topic that hung in the air but finally I asked when Freddy was coming back. 'I wouldn't know,' he said. 'He didn't even tell me he was going.'

On my way out this morning, I was delighted to see a letter for me on the hall table addressed in Alan's handwriting. While he was away at the war, Alan wrote occasionally and Father and I devoured his letters, reading them over and over. He has a dry wit and his stories were full of wonderful observations and insights. I had a few moments to spare and took the letter outside in the sun to relish. My heart sank at the first line. It was evident that this was not a genuine letter from my brother but one transparently dictated by his overbearing wife. The upshot was that Ruth's sister and husband were interested in buying Linnet Lane and had made an offer to purchase it. This, he assured me, was a simple solution to the problem. The proceeds would be split and my share deposited in a trust fund until my return. I would, he explained, have enough left for a nice little bedsit nearer to Balham village. He had enclosed a document for my signature authorising him to accept the offer and dispose of my home without further consultation. A final betrayal by my beloved but weak brother.

Shaken, I tucked the letter away in my pocket and hurried across to the cottage. I thought I was relatively composed but Mr Brooke picked up the wobble in my voice. He listened patiently while I explained the situation, Ruth's ambitions and how I didn't believe these were Alan's true wishes because he knew Father had wanted me to have the security of the house and (by now there were tears) that I don't want to live in a bedsit!

He shrugged dismissively. 'Don't sign it.'

Perhaps it is in my nature to be cooperative and eager to please, but more likely the result of a lifetime of training by Father because I did feel a tiny thrill at the idea of mounting a rebellion. It faded quickly. 'Alan is a solicitor. I'm sure, under pressure —'

'All right, go in guns blazing then.'

With his support I agreed to push back against Ruth. He dictated a short explanatory note to Mr Hubert instructing him to represent me and 'knock this whole business on the head', referring to the intent expressed in Father's will. I typed up the letter on Mr Brooke's Imperial and enclosed the documentation. It will go off in tomorrow's post. Much as I hate to defy Alan, I would love to see the expression on Ruth's face when she opens a letter from *my* solicitor.

I have been uneasy about Lady Jessica, who is still indisposed. Perhaps that's simply because of my prejudice toward her beastly husband. Mr Farley, who used to be so jittery, seems more relaxed and this evening joined Mr Geraldson and Jonathan out on the patio for port and cigars after dinner. I took a moment to step outside and enjoy the night air myself before going up and over-heard Farley enquiring as to Geraldson's university. Geraldson hesitated and then said, 'Cambridge.' Farley said that he too was a Cantabrigian and asked when Geraldson had attended, but Jonathan interrupted and changed the subject – almost as if to protect Geraldson from Farley's prying.

Fascinating as it was to eavesdrop on this mismatched trio, I took the opportunity to dash upstairs, where I discovered that while Mr Farley enjoys a leisurely evening, he locks up his sick wife!

I tapped several times on the bedroom door and then, hear-ing someone behind me, swung around to see Menna advancing rapidly down the hall sorting through a bunch of keys as she walked. She held my eye as she unlocked the door and, the moment I stepped inside, pulled the door closed behind me.

The room was immaculate and even Lady Jessica looked very neat and tidy lying perfectly still in the bed. She was lipsticked and rouged as if ready for a party but didn't appear to be breath-ing. She was dressed in a rose-coloured silk robe. Her arms lay unnaturally by her sides and when I took her hand it felt warm but quite lifeless. Only when I put my face close to hers did I feel her soft breath on my cheek. I gave her a shake and spoke her name. She slept on. There was an urgent tap on the door that I took to be Menna's warning signal. Before I could decide what to do, the key rattled in the lock. The door flew open and Mr Farley stood in the doorway.

'What the devil are you doing in here?' Without waiting for a response, he strode across the room to check on the patient. 'How *dare* you disturb my wife!'

'I was concerned about her,' I said. 'What's wrong with her?'

'Mind your own damn business. I'll speak to Miss Brooke about this. Get out!'

I didn't need a second invitation and fled upstairs to my room. Menna was nowhere to be seen. I now expect to be summoned in the morning and dismissed. Oh, why did I get involved? Just when things are going so well with Mr Brooke . . .

I heard nothing in the morning but when I returned from the cottage this afternoon Vivian was arranging flowers on the hall table – her favourite ruse to ambush people. She looked up and smiled her gracious smile, so it seemed that Mr Farley had not yet carried through his threat. I took the opportunity to enquire into Lady Jessica's health. Vivian frowned and murmured something about convalescence. She looked a trifle irritated when I persisted. I felt that she wanted to tell me it was none of my business but thought better of it. Since my work with Mr Brooke has started in earnest it seems that my stock has appreciated somewhat.

'Hysteria, I believe,' she said, loosening out the arrangement in a practised manner.

'Hysteria? I'm sure that's not a real illness. Is that what the doctor said?'

She gave me a look of cold disbelief. 'I suggest you concern yourself exclusively with the work you are being paid to do. You're very privileged to be mixing with people of a different class here. Don't take it for granted.' I felt as though I had been slapped. Slapped back into my place.

The records we are putting in order now are those stored in a second bedroom of the cottage. There is no bedroom furniture in the room but dozens of cartons mostly containing papers, and five large cupboards the size of wardrobes. These are placed around the room without any thought of order; in fact, several of them block windows and much of the light. Each cupboard has double doors and all are locked. Mr Brooke has made no reference as to the contents and while I am curious, if anything is clear to me by now, it is that in this household one needs to appear uninterested in order to discover anything of import. One thing I am particularly curious about is the mystery of *Aurélie*. How is it that this perfume for which he is so famous is never mentioned – not by him and not by Vivian?

The month of May here is like late June back home but reliably sunny. By the middle of the day the sun is quite intense and the afternoons linger hot and sultry. Despite the heat this afternoon – or perhaps because of it – Mr Brooke decided he wanted to see his rose garden. This is the first time we have undertaken any sort of excursion. It felt a little strange but he seemed comfortable as he slipped his hand inside my elbow, as though escorting me into the theatre. He instructed me to take the path through the garden behind the cottage and then we followed the track that leads up to the road. A high wall runs for some distance alongside the road. I had noticed it on my occasional rambles but took it to be a neighbouring estate. But today, as we approached, I could smell the heady fragrance of the roses in the air.

He unlocked the gate and had me lock it behind us. 'Tell me what you see,' he said.

I looked around in delight. 'Roses. Hundreds and hundreds of beautiful pink roses.'

He smiled, happy to have it confirmed although the overwhelming scent should be confirmation enough. There was only the one type of bloom and it grew in low unruly bushes, not at all like the standard rose we see at home. These plants, he explained, are *Rose de Mai*, sometimes known as *Rose de Grasse* as this variety thrives on the combination of soil and air here. The fragrance was voluptuous, heavenly. The air seemed to sing with a sweet honeyed scent as if we were swimming in it, tasting, breathing, absorbing it through the skin.

Mr Brooke reached into one of the bushes, felt around for a bloom and tore it from the bush. He caressed it roughly but I realised he was assessing the stage of the flowering. 'My great-grandfather built this garden,' he said. 'The original cultivar was brought over from Turkey and propagated here.' He took my arm and we walked up and down the rough ground between the rows of bushes. He asked me questions such as how many blooms were visible on each bush, the condition of the plants and so on. He was so lively and talkative. 'I didn't harvest last year, I'd lost the heart for it,' he said. 'This year I will. This year will be my last harvest.'

'Why the last?'

'They need replanting every ten years. This will be the end of it for me.'

Then he was suddenly in a rush to return to the house, saying he needed to speak to Didier – Monsieur Lapointe – to arrange for pickers. The minute we got back to the cottage he telephoned and was assured that pickers could be brought in as early as Sunday morning. He was most pleased and insisted we have a drop of champagne to celebrate.

I had the one small glass, not wanting a repeat of the last disaster, but still felt cheerfully tipsy as I took my bath before dinner and wafted down to the dining room. So it was a nasty shock to be confronted by the sight of Vivian beetling furiously up the hall toward me. 'How did you get into Mr Farley's room? Do you have a key? Who gave it to you?'

'It was unlocked,' I said (technically true). 'I just went in to see —'

'You seem to have no sense of decorum at all. I made it clear to you from the outset that I had to have implicit trust in you. You have now breached that trust. I am very, *very* disappointed in you. One more incident and your post here will be terminated immediately without notice.' With that, she stormed off into the library where the guests were having their pre-dinner sherry and moments later I heard her tinkling social laughter.

Chapter Seven

Today was the harvest and Mr Brooke had asked if I could come before dawn to take him up to the fields. It was dark as I made my way across the orchard; no need to be discreet at that hour of the morning. I noticed someone moving near the cottage and thought Mr Brooke was likely waiting impatiently for me, although I was early. But the figure was walking toward me and I soon recognised the slow, even gait. It was Menna leaving his house. To avoid me seeing her there? If so, I had thrown the timing out with my promptness. I don't know who I was more disappointed with – she has such dignity and grace – but what do I really know about him? He takes the high ground on issues and seems above reproach. Given his egalitarian claims, you wouldn't pick him as a man who slept with his servant. As it was, she made no effort to avoid me. Our eyes met briefly, as though there is some silent understanding between us. Not a word spoken.

I did feel distinctly odd about it all. I fervently hope that I am not developing feelings for Mr Brooke. I am inclined to harbour secret passions, sometimes without my heart's desire even being aware of my existence. Before the war, the department was populated by young men of varying degrees of attractiveness. I was easily smitten back then. The slightest attention, a kind word or a smile, and I was vividly imagining our courtship and life together. Sooner or later the object of my affection would say or do something disillusioning. Perhaps speak curtly about a tiny typing error (petty) or comment on the size of someone's bosom (vulgar) and our imaginary relationship would be terminated without fuss.

Early on there was a fellow who worked in the auditing section of the department. He invited me to a film on the pretext that the heroine's name was Iris. It was a romantic thriller everyone was talking about at the time called *The Lady Vanishes* directed by Mr Hitchcock. We had a lovely evening and talked about the film for ages in the pub. Then the next week we saw an exhibition at the Tate. So it seemed to be going well. I was not yet twenty with no real experience with men and I yearned to be kissed. I had high hopes that our relationship would blossom and dreamed of the day he would take me in his arms and we would be swept up in our passion. When he did finally make his move it was clumsy and fierce, more like a precursor to a wrestling hold and I resisted – perhaps a little too forcibly. He was shy and took it badly. We walked home in embarrassed silence. It was as though he had done something untoward instead of something quite natural but poorly executed. I didn't know how to clear up the misunderstanding. There were no further invitations and, the next thing I knew, people in his section were going for drinks to celebrate his engagement. It was disappointing but it wasn't the end of the world. I thought there would be other eligible men but the great tide of war came and swept most of them away.

Back to the harvest. I arrived at the cottage to find Mr Brooke pulling on his jacket and raring to go. He was in fine spirits as we set off with a torch up the path toward the rose fields. We could hear the sounds of a truck and voices before we reached the road. Monsieur Lapointe held a lantern to direct a van reversing through the gates into the field. A truck arrived carrying a couple of dozen people, gypsies by the look of them, with ragged children and dogs tagging along. They climbed down, throwing sacks off the back, lighting lanterns, calling out to each other in an exotic-sounding language I didn't recognise.

Monsieur Lapointe came over and talked briefly to Mr Brooke. I gathered that he had inspected the crop yesterday and was enthusiastic about the quality. Although they speak too rapidly for me to follow, I could tell by the warmth in Mr Brooke's responses that he was cheered by this report. Monsieur Lapointe went off to supervise the pickers while we made our way through the gates and found a bench against the stone wall.

Mr Brooke was keen to know what was happening and I attempted to describe the unfolding scene, hoping my commentary in some way resembled his memories of all the harvests he must have witnessed. The flickering lanterns suspended on poles and scattered through the meadow like tiny stars in the pearly grey dawn were quite enchanting. The first blush of light in the sky revealed the pickers in more detail. The women, in long skirts and headscarves, had spread themselves evenly throughout the field. With casual expertise they worked each bush over thoroughly, rapidly plucking blossom after blossom with one hand and pushing a handful at a time into burlap bags slung around their waists. As soon as the bag was full they would untie it and hand it to one of the men, who passed it onto a big fellow with a handlebar moustache who seemed to be in charge and swapped the full bags for empty ones. He took the bags of roses and emptied them into sacks in the back of his van.

By the time the morning sun tipped over the trees it was finished. The gypsies, their children and dogs wandered out and climbed onto the back of the truck. The sounds of their laughter and chatter gradually dwindled as they drove off into the dawning day. When they were gone, the moustached man secured all the sacks in his van and came over to pay his respects to Mr Brooke. Finally he too drove off and the only thing remaining in the garden was the fragrance, thick and opulent in the morning air.

Still no sign of Her Ladyship, which does concern me. On the upside Mr Brooke has been in good spirits since the harvest last week. The roses are now being processed in a factory in Grasse and in time will be returned to him as rose absolute.

Yesterday he decided we should take a break from the endless paperwork and audit the storeroom behind the cottage. We spent several hours ensconced in there, him perched on a high stool directing me to reorganise and document the various raw materials: containers of oils and boxes of equipment such as empty bottles, vials, pipettes and the like. The more light in a room, the easier it is for him to discern shapes but in the dim storeroom he was quite lost and quickly frustrated.

I have never before spent so much time alone with a man in such close proximity. The day was hot and, despite the door being open, we were soon both perspiring. The smell of his mas-culine sweat was a little intoxicating and in some way disturbed my perception of him. I found myself acutely aware of him phys-ically. He would get up from his perch, feel around in various boxes, impatient to know what the contents were. Our bodies touched as we brushed past one another. Fumbling through boxes, our hands would meet. It was a relief to get out of there into the open air, and escape the strange, disturbing intimacy of the confined space.

Working closely with him, I have now come to realise that he is, in fact, extremely orderly and fastidious and the reason for the disorder in his home is solely his blindness. It must be quite discouraging and unsettling for him to know that he exists in a sea of chaos that he is powerless to control.

Once the work was over, I made some tea and we sat in the garden in the late afternoon sun. As we edge into full summer the garden is increasingly fragrant and I keep him up to date with the latest blossoming and the profusion of wildflowers that now carpet the garden.

'It was my great-grandmother who planted this garden,' he volunteered. 'I expect you know that story.' I said I did not and he gave a grunt either of approval or disbelief, but went on to explain that his great-grandfather, Monsieur Rousseau, had built the villa in 1862 when he established the perfume business. When he died the property and business passed to his son (Mr Brooke's grandfather), who built the cottage for his widowed mother while he and his family occupied the main house. The cottage was her home for thirty years and the garden her passion.

By virtue of remaining quietly interested, I was then provided with more information. Mr Brooke revealed that he had been born in England, where his British father had a successful spice importing business. Although his mother died when he was only seven years old, he had vivid memories of her laboratory in their Richmond home and the strange and wonderful smells that emanated from it. Having the misfortune to marry an Englishman, his mother had lived in London under sufferance. She loathed everything about England, but particularly the smells. She loved to motor and several times a year would make the arduous journey from London to the South of France, driving herself and taking the young Hammond with her. It was on one of these trips that she was killed in a motoring accident. Asleep at the time, he escaped unharmed, physically at least.

'My father had been sent away to school at a similar age,' he said. 'I expect he wanted me to suffer the same indignities. Every term break, my grandfather would send a driver for me. So all my summers were spent here.'

'It's a wonderful place for a child,' I said, imagining the fresh and fragrant air as opposed to the dreadful 'pea soup' smogs we have in London now.

He gave a dry laugh. 'I wasn't here to enjoy my childhood, I was here to learn the family trade. Once I turned twelve, my grandfather took me to the factory every day.'

'That doesn't sound terribly much fun for a child.'

'Yes and no. It was in my blood. At the risk of sounding arrogant, I already had the gift, so I was interested. I hated school and preferred it here where I was treated like a little prince – the heir to the throne, so to speak.' He smiled a princely smile. 'I was fourteen when the Great War broke out, and my grandfather refused to send me back to England so I stayed on in France then.'

'What about Vivian?' I asked.

'What about her?'

'Was she sent away to school?'

'How the devil should I know?' he snapped. 'Ask her!'

It really doesn't pay to ask questions, particularly about Vivian. The second my curiosity gets the better of me he gets so furious. I need to watch myself; stay alert.

I'm still shaking as I write this. The most horrible, frightening incident this evening.

After dinner was over, I had only been in my room a few minutes when there was a gentle tap on the door. I opened it to find Lady Jessica half sliding down the door frame. I helped her across my bed. She looked terribly wan, and was begging pitifully for help.

Any thoughts of the trouble I could be in for harbouring her – when I had been told quite clearly not to involve myself – flew out of my head. She had come to me so I was duty-bound to help her. But this was the first place Farley would look for her. Before I could point this out, she fell instantly back to sleep. It was up to me to think of a solution. My first thought was the linen hamper where I had found refuge from Farley, but that was a short-term remedy and even I know that dumping a marchioness in a hamper is inappropriate. Who could I possibly turn to? Menna was obviously already concerned about Lady Jessica but it would be too risky to involve her. The other possibility was Mrs Somerville, who has a soft spot for Lady J.

Locking my door behind me, I rushed downstairs. Mr Farley was still enjoying his nightcap with Jonathan and the place now reeked with the pong of cigar smoke. There was no sign of Mrs S downstairs. I knocked at her door and she called out, 'What is it?' in her usual peremptory tone.

'It's Iris.' After a puzzled silence, I added. 'Miss Turner.'

The door opened and she was no less intimidating in a robe with half a head of curlers. She read something in my expression and invited me in. I quickly described the situation and my suspicions about Mr Farley keeping his wife drugged and captive. Her face darkened. 'Bring her here. I'll take care of her.' When I explained that Lady Jessica was barely conscious, Mrs S, quite the woman of action, threw a coat over her robe and with stealth and speed we rushed up to the top floor.

Lady Jessica remained in a deathlike slumber as we manhandled her out of my room and onto the landing. Mrs Somerville propped her up while I checked the coast was clear. In her pink silk gown, she was like a floppy, slippery sack as we carried her down the stairs to Mrs Somerville's room. We deposited her on the chaise lounge which was a perfect fit. I was surprised by Mrs Somerville's tenderness as she tucked one of her pillows under Lady J's head and drew a blanket over her. Realising Farley would soon be on his way upstairs. I ran back up to my room, pulled on my nightgown and slipped into bed.

I soon heard the doors of empty rooms down the hall slamming, one after the other. He was looking for me and in a temper by the sound. I opened my door, feigning sleepiness, to find him incandescent with rage. He shoved me into the room, pinning me against the wall with his hand tight around my throat – choking me! I was paralysed with terror. 'Where is she? Where is she?' After a moment, I felt almost calm; more than anything, struck by the irony that his nasty face would be my last sight of this world. All strength drained from my limbs. An inky blackness flooded my vision as though falling asleep. All at once his head jerked toward me. His eyes bulged in shock. The hand on my throat fell away as he slumped to the floor. I collapsed, gasping lungfuls of air and coughing – my windpipe still felt compressed. In the silence that followed, I sensed the presence of someone else in the room and looked up to see Menna standing there, her hand still balled in a fist.

So, for the second time tonight, I was helping carry an unconscious person downstairs. The Farleys are not exactly an advertisement for the joys of marriage. Although he was heavier than his wife, Menna is strong – strong enough to knock a man out, so it appears – and we managed him fairly easily. Without ceremony, we took off his clothes and rolled him into bed in his underwear. I tucked him in tightly in the hope he would wake up tomorrow and think it had all been a bad dream. Horrible, horrible man.

I feel such overwhelming gratitude to Menna. He had taken leave of his senses. She saved my life. As we parted on the landing, I caught her wrist. '*Merci. Merci, mon amie.*' She stared at my hand with a worried expression. She looked up at me and smiled. We shared a moment of silent understanding between two women for whom there is little comfort and affection in this world. I suspect she has been through something dreadful. Something that tore her voice from her throat. I feel such a sense of compassion for her. I will be a friend to her.

Truly, what a night! Who knows what tomorrow will bring?

Today began peacefully with only myself and Mr Geraldson at breakfast, which suited me after the drama of last night and disturbed sleep. I suspected this would be my last meal here. Farley may not have known who knocked him out cold but there was no question I was the chief suspect in his wife's disappearance. I knew there was no way to escape Vivian's wrath and my dismissal was looming. But that was not the way things turned out.

The first sign of what was to come was a disturbing tension in the air followed by a complex amalgam of smells that could have been interpreted as distress – hysteria, even – or anger and exasperation. I wasn't overly concerned; the latter are emitted by Vivian regularly over the course of a day. But then came a distant scream from the direction of the kitchen. A glimpse of Vivian's ashen face as she rushed past the door – followed by Dr Renaud. Menna appeared in the doorway like a shadow. I saw the terror in her eyes.

Geraldson woke up to the fact that something was amiss. He put down his newspaper and rose to his feet just as Jonathan rushed in and delivered the shocking news. Mr Farley was *dead*!

There is no doubt in my mind that Farley was alive when we left him. For some reason he did not survive the night. All I can think is that perhaps the blow caused a reaction in his brain from the concussion. Whatever it was, he was discovered dead this morning by Mrs Somerville, who was apparently being treated for shock by the doctor.

'What was Mrs Somerville doing in his room?' asked Geraldson, annoyed by this anomaly.

'It seems his wife slept in the old girl's room last night,' said Jonathan.

'Did Lady Jessica say why?'

'She's still asleep,' said Jonathan.

'No one thought to wake her and break the news?' asked Geraldson.

But then Vivian was calling Jonathan's name and he hurried off, leaving Geraldson none the wiser. Within an hour or so, two men arrived in a black van and took the late Mr Farley away. All I can do is hope and pray that they will not do a postmortem. Yet how could it be otherwise, when yesterday Farley was a healthy specimen in middle age?

I wanted to go straight down and tell Mr Brooke about Farley but we were all instructed by Vivian – in a state of extreme agitation, of course – to gather in the drawing room and not to discuss the situation. The police were coming straight up from Nice to conduct initial interviews so perhaps they already suspected foul play.

So there we all were: Vivian, Jonathan, Mrs Somerville (still shaken), Mr Geraldson, Monsieur Lapointe, Amandine, Madame Bouchard and myself. No Menna or Lady Jessica. We were unhappily dispersed throughout the drawing room like the cast of a stage play waiting for the latest script to be delivered. In Miss Christie's stories the guests are assembled to hear Monsieur Poirot wrap up the case and deliver the final twist. Our situation could have been rather entertaining had one not been quite so involved in the lead-up to Farley's death. As it was, the wait was nerve-racking. I was conscious of the bruising on my neck – which I had masked with a scarf – and a residual huskiness in my voice that could be passed off as a sore throat. These were just my guilty thoughts – it's not as though anyone would suspect the dead man had, earlier in the evening, tried to choke me.

It was an odd situation for the servants to be lumped in with guests and the general sense of discomfort was palpable. Vivian sat perched on the arm of a chair, smoking anxiously. Jonathan circled the drinks trolley but each time he made a determined move toward it, Vivian shot him such a nasty look he recoiled and resumed his pacing. Geraldson stood gazing out the window, chain-smoking in his composed, detached way. Amandine tried to comfort Madame Bouchard, who was crying. She is highly strung at the best of times – it was probably her scream heard earlier. I can't honestly say I'm all that upset about Farley. He was a nasty piece of work and his demise solves so many problems. That sounds horribly callous and mercenary but even the experience of us being 'held for questioning' would be infinitely worse if Farley were here with us, banging on about the Empire.

During our long and increasingly disagreeable wait, the only welcome distraction occurred when Lady Jessica, still in her robe, wandered into the room looking dazed but very refreshed – understandably. Face scrubbed clean, she looked barely out of her teens. 'How perfectly lovely to see everyone gathered together,' she said, gazing around the room with delight. 'What a beautiful day outside!' Clearly our sleeping beauty had not been advised she was lately a widow, although I doubt even that would have dulled her radiance at finding herself splendidly conscious.

Mrs Somerville and Vivian exchanged glances. Vivian looked away and said nothing. I expect she decided to leave it to the police to break the news. Mrs Somerville patted the space beside her on the settee and Lady J settled down to wait, seemingly without curiosity as to the occasion.

Two policemen finally arrived. Vivian met with them for a few minutes and returned to address our group. She explained, first in French, then in English, that we would be asked to go into her office one at a time, after which we were free to go – unless told otherwise. Lady Jessica was the first to go in and Mrs Somerville was next. While we waited, Madame Bouchard stopped crying and reverted to her usual curmudgeonly persona. In a challenging tone, she asked Vivian something, which I gathered, was about Menna. Vivian went over and spoke to her in a quiet, firm voice but the cook was having none of it. Vivian stood her ground, unleashing her death stare. The cook, like most of us, was no match for that and capitulated with an aggressive '*Puurff*'. I heard Vivian repeat one word several times and made a mental note. I had been passing the time browsing the bookshelves so took the opportunity to consult the French–English dictionary. The word she used was '*mutisme*' – mute.

Finally, it was my turn. Back in the scolding chair and even more intimidating than being cross-examined by Vivian. One of the policemen was rather handsome and spoke good English but with a heavy accent that required some concentration to decipher. I was pleased to hear myself answering his questions in a steady, calm voice. The other detective, an older swarthy fellow, spoke no English. He prompted the handsome chap with questions but seemed dissatisfied by every answer. I told the story that would presumably correlate with Mrs Somerville's – which was the truth. Since she knew nothing of the aftermath there was no risk there. Both officers were clearly unhappy with my explanation as to why, when Lady Jessica came to my door and asked for help, I didn't fetch her husband or at the very least take her back to her room. I offered some vague comments about her needing a woman's care – hoping this would be interpreted as 'women's troubles' because I wasn't sure how far Mrs Somerville might have gone in accusing Farley of drugging his wife.

'You are a friend of Madame Farley?' the handsome fellow asked in a way that appeared both sympathetic and interested. 'Perhaps she speak of troubles with her 'usband?'

I was especially careful with my responses to these ambiguous questions and avoided expressing any opinion about the Farleys or the state of their marriage. I can only hope Vivian doesn't reveal that he had recently made a complaint about my interference. Fortunately all evidence of the earlier shoe-throwing incident has died with him.

Menna and I had left the Farleys' room unlocked in case he didn't have a key and woke up to find himself inexplicably locked in his own room. So when asked about this (in a roundabout way), I was careful not to speculate or justify anything relating to the keys, merely saying that security was not an issue in the house – the implication being that an unlocked door would not be unusual. I am almost certain that's what the others will say.

Finally I was released and able to rush down to the cottage and tell Mr Brooke the story. Not the whole story, obviously. If it was Menna's blow that killed Farley, her secret will go with me to the grave. I realise there is a risk writing all this down but if I am to remain composed on the surface, I need to pour it out somewhere. After a lengthy exploration of my room I have found the perfect hiding spot for my journal in a gap behind the skirting board. The contents could now be deadly. A convicted murderer in France would face death by guillotine.

The atmosphere in the house has been subdued and Vivian in such a temper one daren't even speak to her, but Lady Jessica resembles a butterfly liberated from her chrysalis. Once the post-mortem is complete and Farley's body released, she plans to return to England by aeroplane for the funeral – accompanied by none other than Mrs Somerville! Over the last couple of days, the two of them have become inseparable. One can see them at different times of the day strolling in the garden, playing mahjong in the drawing room or taking tea on the verandah, as though enjoying a delightful holiday together. Lady Jessica seems entirely happy apart from the occasional tearful moment that may be related to grief or possibly whatever she endured at Farley's brutish hand. In my short experience of Mrs Somerville I have never seen her happier either, now she has both a purpose and a protégée.

Chapter Eight

Dr Renaud has come to see Mr Brooke several times a week lately. They are good friends so these are social visits as well as medical ones. Father Furolo, the Italian priest, also visits him regularly in the evenings. I suspect those visits are not so much pastoral care, more an opportunity to debate the woes of the world over whisky and cigars. But this afternoon Monsieur Lapointe took Mr Brooke into Marseille for a medical appointment. Something is going on but he hasn't said a word to me.

With an afternoon to myself, I decided to make a start on *Madame Bovary*, borrowed from Vivian's library. Quite an undertaking and indication of my sense of optimism for my future here. I settled myself out on the patio in the shade of the bougainvillea, now smothered with scarlet blossoms, and had barely finished the first line when I was joined by Mrs Somerville, who rang the bell for Amandine to bring coffee and biscuits. Despite the interruption it was a beautiful afternoon and very pleasant to be relaxing outside. Mrs Somerville had, as she phrased it, 'put Lady Jessica down for a nap', which seemed an extraordinary thing to say about a grown woman. She does adore fussing over her new friend.

'The English aristocracy are feudal – so behind the times,' announced Mrs Somerville. 'That poor girl was practically traded – like a horse – to that monster. People think England is a civilised country but it's still in the dark ages. Barbaric.'

Barbaric? Not sure if she realised I am actually English, I suggested that she was perhaps overstating it a little.

'Not at all,' she said darkly. 'What that girl has had to put up with. Practically prisoner to a man with *excessive sexual appetites*.' She enunciated this last part with some relish. 'Poor dear child.'

My eyes wandered back to *Madame Bovary* in the vain hope she would not share further intimate confidences.

'Honey, would you like to join us this afternoon? We're going down to Nice to buy Jessie a few little French outfits to take home. We'll stop in for a cocktail somewhere and be back in time for dinner. What do you say?'

'Oh, I don't think —'

'Come on, why not?' she said. 'You haven't been out for weeks.'

It was true. Apart from the occasional walk, I had barely left the place. I supposed *Madame Bovary* could wait another day.

Mrs Somerville had made her own transport arrangements and a uniformed driver arrived on the dot of three in a large black Mercedes and swept us off to Nice.

There was a mood of celebration in the car – relief at escaping the oppressive atmosphere of the house, I expect. Lady Jessica wore a frilly frock and Mrs Somerville an indulgent smile. Lady J is giddy at the best of times and seems to find Mrs Somerville's brittle attempts at humour wildly amusing. They made quite a pair.

They will have to sober up somewhat back in England. It wouldn't do for Her Ladyship to be so deliriously happy at her late husband's funeral.

Shopping in Nice could have been a pleasant experience but was made tedious by Mrs Somerville's extravagant pampering of Lady Jessica. Being dragged in and out of ruinously expensive shops, where her every whim was satisfied, I felt like the orphan child tagging along to provide contrast. Everything was paid for by Mrs Somerville since the young widow apparently has not a penny of her own. Never mind that she brought trunks full of clothes with her when she arrived.

Finally we retired to the sumptuous lounge of Hôtel Le Negresco, leaving our poor driver, who had patiently followed us around all afternoon collecting the booty, sitting outside in the car. Mrs Somerville immediately ordered 'the best champagne you have' in an unnecessarily loud voice and I wished profoundly to be somewhere quiet in the company of *Madame Bovary*. The hotel is decorated in an extravagant *Belle Époque* style with footmen decked out in eighteenth-century livery – excessive to my simple tastes. However, Mrs Somerville gazed around with great satisfaction and pronounced the place 'classy', which Lady Jessica found hilarious, causing me to wonder if that sleeping draught had caused long-term damage. Further confirmation came when, quite out of the blue, she announced furiously that she had *never* liked France. 'I detest the French. And that policeman was terribly rude to me. I do hope they finish with Douglas soon. I simply can't wait to get home to England.'

Our champagne arrived and we raised our glasses to Lady Jessica's future, which seemed to calm her down. I noticed a well-dressed couple wander into the foyer from the opposite bar.

It took a moment to realise it was Topsy and William. Although I was side-on to them, I knew Topsy had seen me as the lobby area was reflected quite clearly in the mirror to my right. For a moment, she dithered. There was a discussion and it seemed William was the reluctant one. But Topsy prevailed and they came into the lounge. She kissed me effusively and I made the introductions, explaining that Lady Jessica was recently widowed but Topsy had apparently already heard of Farley's death through the expat grapevine. She was terribly sympathetic.

'What happened to the poor man? Was he ill?' she asked.

'Oh no, he just died,' said Lady Jessica. 'He —'

'We don't know,' interrupted Mrs Somerville. 'There's a post-mortem.'

'How distressing for you,' Topsy said in a faux-sympathetic voice.

The conversation was stilted and uncomfortable as Topsy explained they were just leaving. Mrs Somerville, with typical indiscriminate American hospitality, absolutely insisted they join us and the next thing more glasses and champagne were being delivered. William seemed less than enthusiastic and didn't involve himself in the conversation but Lady Jessica and Topsy were a match made in heaven, chatting away excitedly about various mutual friends in London with Mrs S left out in the cold, conversationally speaking.

In a quiet aside, William asked, 'And what have you been doing today, Miss Turner?'

'Very little. I'm here simply as an audience,' I said. 'To witness and observe.'

'Don't underestimate your value. What is a performer without an audience?'

'I see your point, but I have yet to find anything to applaud.'

He laughed quietly. Topsy glanced over and although she couldn't have heard our exchange, her expression was most intriguing. Considering she had so recently been trying to matchmake us – so I thought – she looked oddly vulnerable, which led me to speculate as to how they came to be here in the hotel on a Friday evening. Perhaps the business of setting me up with William was actually a smokescreen? I confess to a slight pang of disappointment.

'I never expected to find you at this salubrious watering hole, Iris,' said Topsy.

'I insisted,' said Mrs Somerville. 'She never seems to leave the place.'

'Understandably,' replied Topsy. 'There's bound to be a problem when you live and work in the same place.'

'Oh really?' Mrs Somerville looked at me with new curiosity. 'I thought you were a friend of the family. What work do you do?'

Before I could think of how to curtail the conversation, Topsy explained that I worked for Mr Brooke. 'Mr Brooke? There's a Mr Brooke?' asked Mrs Somerville, sounding quite irritable.

'I don't think Mrs Somerville will be interested in all that,' I said.

'I believe he is a recluse, but I'm surprised you haven't met him since he lives on the property.' Topsy gave me a cool smile. She knew perfectly well that she was embarrassing me.

'I've never even set eyes on him,' said Mrs Somerville in wonder.

'You must have heard of him. He's a famous perfumer —' insisted Topsy.

'Famous?'

Topsy tossed back her champagne as if to get down to business.

'Topsy, please, I'd rather you didn't —'

My lame protests were no match for the lure of the spotlight. She leaned toward Mrs Somerville and breathed, '*Aurélie!*'

It is well accepted that Americans have a gift for overreaction, to be utterly repulsed by something mildly disagreeable or turn an incident that might warrant a raised eyebrow into a theatrical event. Mrs Somerville is no exception, and delivered a jaw-dropping parody of shock. She stared at me in wonder, as though my royal origins had been revealed. 'Oh my! She never said a word. I had no idea! Where in the world is he hiding?'

Although by comparison to my involvement in Mr Farley's death, this conversation was a relatively minor problem, there is no doubt that my earlier indiscretion has betrayed Mr Brooke's trust in the worst possible way. I couldn't see any way now to stop Mrs Somerville tackling Vivian and/or taking herself down to the cottage, intent on meeting the great man himself. She is the personification of someone who doesn't take no for an answer.

Lady Jessica, too young to remember *Aurélie* and further confused at no longer being the centre of attention, kept asking what on earth we were talking about. As Mrs Somerville began to explain the situation to her, William glanced over at Topsy and discreetly tapped his watch. She nodded vaguely, loathe to leave the excitement she had generated, but nevertheless gathered herself and said her goodbyes. Once they had departed, Mrs Somerville continued to bother me with questions. I had to be quite firm that Mr Brooke's privacy was paramount and that it would not be possible to meet him – to little effect.

Lady Jessica sulked a little and then said petulantly, 'I don't see why we have to stay here any longer.'

'Oh, let's get back – it's almost dinner time anyway – you're probably hungry,' said Mrs Somerville.

'I hate that house. I wanted to go to Paris. Douglas promised me. Now I'll never go,' said Lady Jessica, seeming to contradict her earlier condemnation of everything French.

'Honey, we can go to Paris anytime you like,' said Mrs Somerville.

'Now? Right this minute?'

I had never heard Mrs Somerville laugh out loud, which in retrospect was a small mercy, because she now issued an eerie braying sound at a volume that brought footmen to the door, no doubt wondering if peacocks were mating in the lounge.

The moment we were back in the car, Lady Jessica – who incidentally speaks quite decent French – informed the driver that they would travel to Paris tonight. He made some grumbling complaints but she took no notice and told Mrs Somerville it was all arranged. Back at the house, both women were in absurdly high spirits running back and forth to each other's rooms like a couple of schoolgirls going off on excursion. They only had room for a single valise each, so much cross-consultation was needed.

Vivian was understandably discombobulated. One guest dead and now this unlikely pair leaving at a moment's notice. Lady Jessica dismissed her earlier plan and decided her husband could travel to England unaccompanied. Mrs Somerville rather indiscreetly handed Vivian a great wad of notes to pay for both their rooms and instructed her to store their trunks until they sent a forwarding address. Finally – to my considerable relief – they bade us farewell and drove off into the night.

The most extraordinary revelation this evening. We are much reduced in numbers at supper with only myself, Mr Geraldson, Jonathan and Vivian – who looked slightly less grim than previous evenings. We had just begun the soup course when she said, 'The police have dropped their investigations. It appears that Mr Farley took his own life.'

While this outcome was an enormous relief, how was that possible? How did he hit himself in the back of the head while in a horizontal position?

'What nonsense! Absurd! Completely absurd,' shouted Jonathan. 'We had a nightcap with him that very evening, didn't we, Geraldson? He was in perfectly good humour —'

'For God's sake, calm down, Jonathan,' Vivian interrupted. 'There were obviously some problems in the marriage for Lady Jessica to run off —'

'Wives are always running off! Besides, she hadn't even left the bloody building!'

Vivian's mouth set in a stubborn line. 'Jonathan, I suggest we leave it to the experts. Better suicide than . . . than the other.'

'How did he supposedly kill himself then?' asked Jonathan.

'Veronal. A bottle on the bedside table. Consistent with the autopsy.'

'It could have been accidental,' said Geraldson. 'Perhaps he didn't measure out the grains carefully enough. Not uncommon.'

'Farley was careful. He was a careful man,' said Jonathan.

'Anyway, that was the finding. Now I suggest we put the

whole ghastly episode behind us,' said Vivian.

'Anyone could have administered it to him while he was asleep – his dim-witted wife, for instance!' said Jonathan.

'She was with Mrs Somerville. The police are satisfied, I don't see why you shouldn't be,' said Vivian.

'Where are you getting all this information? Why are the police reporting to you, anyway? It's not in the papers and it's not as though you're next-of-kin —'

'It comes direct from the *commissaire*.' Vivian's tone was cold steel.

Jonathan stared at her in disbelief. 'Oh, I see what's going on here.' He stood up, knocking his chair over. 'You're *at it* with him now!'

'Jonathan, sit down,' Vivian said. 'Don't be ridiculous. Behave yourself. You're drunk and confused – think of your blood pressure. *Sit down.*'

I sensed Geraldson was rather enjoying himself but I most definitely was not. Amandine stood in the doorway holding an empty tray. She may not have understood the conversation, but the mood needed no interpretation. I hadn't seen Jonathan so animated and he was indeed quite scarlet in the face. At Vivian's command, he sulkily recovered his fallen chair and flopped into it. Amandine took this as a cue to hurriedly collect the soup bowls, despite the fact that none of us had finished. Geraldson pushed back his chair and lit a cigarette, probably to mask that annoying smirk of his.

As I left the dining room after dinner, Vivian followed and caught me on the stair. 'I expect it is crystal clear that you do not breathe a word of that conversation – or anything else that happens in this house. The Riviera is a very small place. I will know.'

I murmured my reassurances but could feel her watching me as I walked self-consciously up the stairs.

'I would prefer you use the service stairs in future,' she called after me. 'The main stair is exclusively for guests.'

I feel nostalgic now for the times when she was so charming to me. Those days are long gone. It's hard to know what I have done to raise her ire, especially now that we are actually making progress with the work – and I am the only person she has hired who has achieved that.

Now I have had some time to think the situation through, it is possible that Farley regained consciousness, realised that his wife had gone, he had disgraced himself attacking a defenceless woman, and impulsively decided to end it all. But I can't see it. He was not the sensitive type, let alone remorseful. I think it more likely that someone else administered it to him while he was out cold.

Mr Brooke has thoroughly relished all the drama up at the house. It seems that Monsieur Lapointe also has some sort of relationship with the *commissaire* (though obviously of a different nature to Vivian's) or perhaps with someone else in the police department, as he had reported back some interesting snippets of information about Mr Farley. One of which was that Farley did not serve his country at all. Throughout the war, he was a guest of His Majesty, interned in Brixton Prison under a wartime regulation that allowed for enemies of Britain to be held without charges or trial.

'I told you I knew that name, Farley,' said Mr Brooke with some satisfaction. 'Typical of Vivian to be busy cultivating a nest of fascists up there.'

'I don't know that you can call one man a nest, exactly.'

'What about Geraldson? What have you found out about him?'

I was about to remind Mr Brooke that I had turned down the role of informant when a penny dropped. 'Actually, although he goes to some lengths to disguise the fact, I think he's German.'

'What did I tell you?'

'That doesn't automatically make him fascist,' I pointed out.

'What do you mean by "some lengths"?'

There wasn't much to go on and I had to admit there was no real reason for him to pretend to be British. Germans were hardly popular in France since the occupation but he didn't seem like a man who cared about popularity. I shared my theory that he is here on business as he often goes away for several days at a time but then returns.

'I've got a pretty good idea who he is,' Mr Brooke said. 'It's bloody frustrating knowing there are people up there plotting against me – not being able to find out what the hell is going on.'

'What do you mean? How are they plotting against you?'

'This Geraldson practically lives there and yet no one seems to know a thing about him. He's part of her scheme, I'm certain of it.'

'Vivian's scheme?'

He stopped himself with a stubborn jut of the jaw so I diverted the conversation onto the tasks for the day. In fact, he is still quite invigorated about the work and suggested that, as the paperwork is almost under control, we should move on to sorting out the cupboards in that second bedroom. The air in this room is so drenched with scent it is as though you're breathing a dense fragrant soup. This is where the core of Mr Brooke's frustration and anger resides. It has a dark, crowded atmosphere with a large cluttered desk against one wall, the imposing cupboards standing sentry and more cartons of materials stacked on the floor. I opened a window but this did little to lighten or ventilate the room. Mr Brooke navigated the many obstacles effortlessly, giving the impression he often wandered around in there. I hope not to spend too much time in that oppressive environment.

He unlocked one of the cupboards to reveal it was packed with dozens of small bottles of raw ingredients. Far from the evocative floral titles one might expect, the labels consisted only of codes. He asked me to read some of them to him. It is hard to imagine how a series of numbers and letters could bring such pleasure but it was as though I were reading poetry aloud. The tension in his face eased, and he gazed into the middle distance with a fond smile.

The plan was for me to read out each code. He would then divulge the actual contents of the bottle which I would record in a ledger and then type up an inventory of all his raw materials.

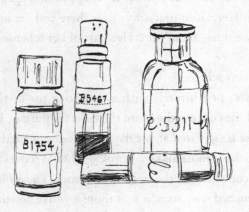

There was something perplexing about this process and there's the question of why the contents and codes are not already cross-referenced and documented. Did he create this code system and commit it to memory for reasons of secrecy? And will this inventory actually be handed over to Vivian? He had me fetch some crates and straw from the storeroom for packing. It was going to be a long, slow process and I could sense his reluctance as we began – this is the heart and soul of his business we will now pack away.

He made himself comfortable in his old swivel chair while I did the legwork getting out the bottles and cross-referencing the codes against the contents. It seems inconceivable that he could have all these hundreds of codes in his head but he does. Given each code, he responded without hesitation, naming bergamot, tuberose, freesia, neroli, gardenia, ylang-ylang, sandal-wood, cedarwood – and these are only the more common ones I can recall now. Perhaps he sensed this was an arduous chore for me, and one that will take weeks. When he suggested that I uncap F5364 and smell it, it was as though he wanted to share his almost religious reverence and affection for these materials so essential to his craft.

'What are you getting?' he asked.

'Is it . . . magnolia?'

'No, what do *you* get?'

I don't usually do requests but decided to indulge him. 'Perseverance.'

'Anything else?'

'I suppose . . . dignity, graciousness?'

'Interesting. Now try B5467.'

I located the bottle, uncapped it and took a breath. 'Violet.'

'And?'

I inhaled once more, allowing my instincts to do the work. 'Loyalty. Faithfulness.'

'Incredible. I've been remiss in not saying this before, but I have never known anyone with such a unique gift for interpretation.'

'I have never considered it a gift, it's simply one of my senses.'

'I know we discussed this briefly but it seems to me that you can sense the vibrations within a smell and then intuit one step further. You have the ability to absorb subtle emotions or moods and store the memories. You're identifying something in these fragrances that is implicit. Deeply embedded in an almost mystical way. It's quite extraordinary.'

'But you have this gift,' I said.

'What makes you say that?' His tone had a hard edge to it. It was now or never.

'Because you created *Aurélie*.'

He was silent for a long moment. Sorrow crept into the room like a salty mist. It was as though I had mentioned someone who had passed on. Someone he was still grieving for. 'Tell me what you smelled in *Aurélie*.'

I thought back to my initial impressions. Colleen had been the first person in the department to own a bottle. She had always been a kind and generous person but it seemed to me that when she began to wear this fragrance her virtues were brought to the fore, highlighted in a way that abrogated any faults or failings. The fragrance seemed to herald her natural goodness and other people recognised her attributes. I tried to isolate that memory from my experience. To recapture the moment when I smelled it in its purest form. 'Promise,' I said. 'It was an evocation of the promise in each of us.'

To my surprise, his eyes filled with tears. It was so unexpected I barely knew what to say. The room filled with a deep silence. Outside the day was fading, the golden light of the afternoon sliding away, leaving shadow in its path.

'You must have an extraordinary sense of smell to create a fragrance like *Aurélie*.'

'I did once. It's gone.'

'Gone?' I couldn't have been more shocked.

'Like my blindness, anosmia is associated with my condition. I'm gradually losing all my senses to this bastard diabetes. My nose is just a structure on my face now. Redundant.'

It seems inconceivable that Mr Brooke's greatest gift has been stolen from within. Now I understand his anger. I told him how very sorry I was. No words could do the situation justice. After a time he said, 'Before we pack all this up, let's make one last fragrance. Together.'

'My sense is undisciplined. It's just instinct. I don't have any skills.'

'I'll guide you. We will make it very simple.' He then sat thinking for so long I worried he would change his mind. 'This composition will be made for you. It will be everything the world needs to know about you.' He smiled. 'It will be the essence of Iris.' He gave a chuckle. 'We can call it *Iridescence*.'

And so we started.

The day faded into evening. Menna brought food and slipped away. Our task was completely engrossing, almost like a mathematical abstraction that starts with a concept and works its way toward a resolution through trial and error, defined not by numbers but by smell. Mr Brooke still has the ability to derive something from nothing, from vibrations, as he puts it.

He insisted that the fragrance should highlight my less obvious attributes. He noted my sense of humour, intelligence and empathy but also honesty and courage. Wonderful attributes I am not entirely sure I possess! I went along with him because it was making him so happy and I was touched that he had observed these qualities in me.

He pondered each of my traits long and hard before giving me the code and the exact amount to measure into the beaker. I made a careful note of each element and quantity, some of which played a major role; others were minuscule.

It was a laborious but fascinating process that involved regular rethinking and reworking. Over the last few days we have continued our work on the stocktake but his mind has been constantly drawn back to the composition, reminding me that each manifestation is a draft still to be perfected. Over and over he asked me to dip a test strip into the formulation and explain it to him. Sometimes I had to leave the cottage and stand outside in the fresh air to clear my senses. In the normal scheme of things he would create these compositions over weeks or months, reflecting on each draft and reworking it. But our time is limited.

By the time the final composition of *Iridescence* was decanted into a bottle we were both exhausted and exultant. How to find words to describe it? There is no sense of it conforming with the usual fragrance structures. It's not definable as fruity or floral or citrus, etcetera, but all those elements are present in some form. As with *Aurélie* the emphasis is not on the fragrance itself but what it brings to the surface. It may be quite different for someone else, but for me *Iridescence* is a distillation and compression of every memory of happiness in my life. It's the scent of contentment.

It was late this evening when we finished. I packed up the plates from the final meal Menna had brought over and had begun to wash them up when she arrived back at the cottage. I felt a little awkward at her presence but she smiled at me warmly and seemed quite relaxed about me being there. She fetched a small black bag down from the kitchen cupboard, laid the contents on the bench and went about some preparations I couldn't observe without being obvious.

Mr Brooke bade me goodnight and went to his room. Menna followed him in and closed the door. I had seen her discard something in the bin and went over to look. I feel such a fool. I pride myself on picking up on subtleties but so often miss what is blindingly obvious. It was an empty insulin vial.

Chapter Nine

Alexander rang to invite me out dancing this evening and even though I'm a mediocre dancer with a small repertoire, I was delighted to accept after a week of hard work. The choice of wardrobe was limited to my violet taffeta, rather old-fashioned, but it has a nice full skirt. Some crystal beads would have added a little sparkle but I only had a strand of pearls that once belonged to my mother. All was redeemed by a dab of *Iridescence* that made me feel more glamorous than my dress really allowed for. The whole effect was considerably dampened by my cardigan and lumpy purse, but I doubted anyone would notice. Being inconspicuous does have advantages.

Leaving via the back stair, I bumped into Menna. She gave me an appraising look and beckoned me to follow her. She led me downstairs to a box room off the service hall where the trunks left behind by Lady Jessica and Mrs Somerville were stored. Menna undid the straps of a large leather trunk. Inside, all was beautifully neat and tidy. Given that Lady Jessica had left in such a rush, this was presumably Menna's handiwork. She carefully lifted various items out until she found a cream stole. I discarded the offending cardigan and she draped the stole around my shoulders – heavenly, like a cloud of cashmere. Next were some long white evening gloves and a pretty beaded purse in silver and cream. I went along to the servants' bathroom to admire myself. It may have been the dingy light and mottled-looking glass, but the image that materialised looked quite lovely.

At my discreet request (bypassing Vivian), Monsieur Lapointe agreed to chauffeur me down to Cannes where I was to meet Alexander. To my delight, when we pulled up outside the Carlton Hotel the doorman hastened to open my door as he had for those more illustrious guests. Monsieur Lapointe, who had maintained his smouldering silence throughout the trip, glanced over his shoulder and gave me a nod – it may be too far-fetched to say it was of approval, but at least of acknowledgement.

On my first visit to the Carlton I was too shy to enter the hotel and skulked around outside like a child afraid to go into the classroom. Now here I was swanning into the foyer like a *bona fide* guest! I went through into the bar as instructed and found Alexander, who had secured a table and already drunk half a bottle of expensive champagne. I expected him to be dazzled by my borrowed finery and looked forward to some compliments. He didn't notice, only asking if I was suitably shod for the dance floor.

'Perfectly,' I assured him. 'But I have so much to tell you first. I expect you've heard about Mr Farley's demise?'

'Who hasn't? Seemed very suspicious to me. I expect the only reason the police aren't investigating any further is because they think the British aristocracy could do with culling. Minor aristocracy, I should add.'

'It's all come out now that he was a fascist.'

'Who isn't?' he said. 'No reason to go murdering a chap. Although by all accounts he sounded like a nasty little toad.'

There were so many things I was bubbling to tell him but remembered just in time that Alexander can be terribly indiscreet. I couldn't resist sharing the news that Mr Brooke had created a perfume for me.

'Oh, has he now? I expect the old goat has designs on you. Actually, you do look rather ravishing tonight. Although I quite miss your usual frumpiness; I find it comforting. It reminds me of Nanny.'

Alexander likes to be witty at other people's expense and, depending on the victim, it can sometimes be amusing. But tonight his catty comment hit me hard. A minute before I had felt lovely and glamorous, perfectly at ease in this sumptuous hotel. Now I felt like a foolish frump. A sow's ear. I felt a wave of fury that he could puncture my confidence so easily, so thoughtlessly. Without a moment's consideration I picked up my champagne glass and flung the contents into his face. Never in my entire life have I done anything so impetuous and silly, but it was worth it for his expression of utter astonishment. I could feel all eyes were on us and I didn't care. I pulled my stole firmly around my shoulders and stalked out, straight through the front doors and across the road to the bay.

Anyone watching the last three minutes of my life would imagine I'm one of those prima donna types who doesn't put up with any nonsense. In truth I was racked with self-recrimination. What makes people think they can be so rude to me? Do I exhibit a bovine acceptance that encourages people to lash out at me with no consideration for my feelings?

I stood on the promenade and gripped the railing, the twilight ocean blurred by angry tears. I had been so looking forward to this evening. Now it was in tatters. I would have to go back to the Carlton and have them telephone the house and ask Monsieur Lapointe to come back and collect me. He would not be in a civil mood having to turn straight around. Better to lash out for a taxi.

Then Alexander appeared at my side. Without a word he wrapped his arms around me and hugged me tightly. I stood helpless in his grip as he placed my floppy arms around his waist in a forced embrace. 'Forgive me. Please. I don't deserve to even be in your presence, let alone have you as a dear friend.'

I pulled away from him and straightened my dress. 'You see, you simply take things too far. You should have stopped at forgive me – that was enough. Then you started being melodramatic. Now I don't believe you're sincere.'

'I am. I was thoughtlessly cruel. I'm truly sorry.'

'Why do people think it's perfectly acceptable to be so horrible to me?'

'Who else is horrible?' He sounded slightly put out, as though it were his prerogative alone.

'You should hear the way Vivian speaks to me.'

He adopted a tragic expression that wasn't terribly convincing but I permitted him to link arms with me and we walked along Boulevard de la Croisette, promenading with other couples dressed for an evening on the town. 'I think it's because you're so inscrutable,' he said after a while.

I had to laugh at the ridiculousness of that explanation. 'Inscrutable?'

'Truly, I've only realised just this moment how evolved you

are. Like someone who has lived for a thousand years and understands the world and can make sense of it.'

'Now you're being fanciful and absurd.'

He stopped and gazed into my face. 'I feel you have been sent to guide me. Like a guardian angel you appeared in my life at a time of complete despair.'

'What despair? Anyhow, it's not as though you take any notice of anything I say.'

'Only because it hadn't struck me before. Now I'm experiencing the most profound epiphany about you!' He laughed his crazy laugh and I couldn't help but laugh too.

We were all right after that. Although it was still early, we went straight to the nightclub. The casino was already doing brisk business. Thankfully we didn't stop in there but went straight up to the cabaret room. The room itself was quite lovely. Old-style French architecture with red velvet curtains framing a large dais where a six-piece band dressed in slick black suits played. An attractive blonde in a red blouse and tight black skirt sang one of those mournful French songs. The dance floor, which was surrounded by tables and chairs, had capacity for a couple of dozen dancers at most. We took a table and Alexander ordered more champagne. His suit still had a few damp spots from the last effort.

'I know it all looks tame right now,' he said, gazing around, 'but it will heat up later on. Topsy and Seb might join us.'

I remember thinking there must be some other people Alexander knows on the Côte d'Azur. I really don't mind Topsy and Sebastian but they are just not my sort of people. They may profess to adore me but that adoration is of, I suspect, something I represent. Hopefully not their nannies. They don't know me at all. I'm certain that when it's time for me to leave, they will be the last to notice I'm gone. If they notice at all.

'What's your best step, my lovely?' Alexander asked when the champagne and cocktail snacks arrived.

'Waltz, foxtrot —' He fought a mocking smile as I went on lamely. 'I could probably manage the merengue.'

One glass of champagne later and I was on the dance floor with Alexander holding me in a hypnotic gaze. '*Un, deux,* cha-cha-cha, turn, two, cha-cha-cha – swivel those hips – oh la la – cha-cha-cha.'

I don't remember when I ever had such terrific fun.

By the time we took a break, the tables and the dance floor were busy. Topsy, Sebastian and William wandered in with Freddy trailing behind them. Alexander waved everyone over to join us at the table and became endearingly animated in the presence of Freddy, who kindly remembered me as Alex's 'clever little friend'.

I felt quite breathless and flushed with the excitement of it all but Freddy gazed around the room with a jaded eye and remarked that he must bring his mother here when she next visited. Alexander assured him that we planned to eat there and go on to another, more lively club that opened after ten. This news was a little disappointing to me but Freddy seemed satisfied with that plan.

We all had to practically shout over the music and the crowd. It was chaotic but great fun. William was unusually attentive. It seemed he was hanging on my every word but perhaps he just found it difficult to hear me over the din. I wasn't holding out any hope in that regard since I had intuited that he and Topsy were involved in some way. I wondered how long it had been going on and whether they were actually in love. That would give Sebastian something to write about if he ever found out.

The food took forever to arrive and was then rather hurried. The dance floor was overflowing and people were bumping into the backs of our chairs. So it was a delight to be released out into the balmy night. We all strolled through the back lanes of Cannes. William walked with me and we enjoyed a relaxed conversation about nothing in particular.

Alexander led us down some steps and through a huge arched doorway into what must have been a wine cellar for a hotel or a large house. Music bounced off the brick walls. The place was heaving, the air dense with cigarette smoke and the altogether thrilling smell of wild abandon. People hurled themselves around in the most frenetic version of the jive I have ever witnessed. (I felt a little foolish in my taffeta and pearls, like a debutante in an opium den.) It was the most lively evening imaginable. The jive was enormously fun and exhausting. First I danced with Alexander, then with Freddy, and then with anyone who pulled me in to dance.

It all became increasingly chaotic. Alexander – who had somehow acquired a bright red fez with a long black tassel – and Freddy added to the pandemonium as they carved a path through the crowd with a highly dramatised version of the tango that was quite hilarious. Topsy had been in a sour mood all evening, bickering with Sebastian. She sat at the bar drinking and smoking unhappily while her husband threw himself into the fray.

William didn't dance but stood alone in the doorway and watched the madness with obvious pleasure. Sometime in the early hours he shouted in my ear that he was leaving and offered to take me home. Although it was doubtless well out of his way,

I accepted gratefully. We walked in silence to his car, music still ringing in our ears. Once in the car, I must have immediately fallen asleep because the next thing I knew he was shaking me gently awake. I apologised for sleeping the entire way home, which he was very gracious about.

He leapt out of the car and opened my door. We said our goodnights but as I went to leave, he pulled me toward him and crushed his lips against mine. It took me completely by surprise but (learning from past errors) I let my body yield to his embrace. His kiss was soft and warm and blissfully delicious. I wanted it never to end. But end it did; its splendour only slightly tarnished by his apology which may have implied it was a mistake. Now, alone in my room, I can't stop touching my lips and smiling in disbelief. I shan't sleep a wink for reliving the experience all night long.

I woke this morning euphoric but am now in my room under orders to pack, as I am leaving.

I had decided – while still in my state of emotional intoxication – that I would not be relegated to the service stair. I don't hold with this upstairs–downstairs elitism. Vivian is living in the past in that regard. As luck would have it, I didn't encounter her during my defiant descent so was not called on to justify my manifesto – the cowardly rebel, that's me!

She was already at breakfast and didn't look up from her newspaper. Jonathan arrived right behind me, pecked her on the cheek and fell into his chair with a great huff.

'Jonathan, pleeeease. Just pull out your chair and sit down like a *normal adult*.' Her voice rose in a vibrato of irritation.

Jonathan apologised and she continued in a calmer tone. 'I have several new guests arriving next week. Two sisters —'

'Not Americans, I hope, I really can't bear them,' Jonathan interrupted.

'I'm not in a position to turn away guests whose nationality displeases you in some way.'

'I don't see why not. I'm easily your most loyal guest.'

Vivian picked up the coffee pot, glanced my way as if to offer some and froze, staring at me. I fingered my hair self-consciously, wondering what on earth had caused such a reaction.

'What have you done to yourself?' She sniffed the air, gently at first, and then like a bloodhound on a trail. 'What's that smell?'

'Good lord, Vivian,' said Jonathan. 'Don't talk to me about manners.'

'What is that perfume?' she demanded.

'Mr Brooke made it for me —'

'Don't be ridiculous, what are you talking about?' Her fury was escalating by the second.

'Well, we made it together . . .' The words faded on my lips.

She stood up slowly, her rage terrifying. 'Go upstairs and pack your bags. You are nothing but trouble.' Leaving that absurd and unfair statement hanging in the air, she walked out the doors to the garden and strode off toward the cottage.

Jonathan and I exchanged looks. He pulled out a hip flask and took a swig. As an afterthought, he wiped off the top and offered it to me. I refused, despite my mortification. 'Do you have any idea why she's so angry?'

'It's a complex situation,' he said, buttering his toast. 'Hmmm, I'm not really privy to the finer details. Suffice to say there's money involved. A great deal of money, I should think.'

'Should I go down there? I mean, Mr Brooke . . .' My voice was thick with sudden tears at the thought of Vivian's rage being directed at him and no one there to defend him. Not that I would be any match for Vivian.

Jonathan looked up slowly from his breakfast and stared at me. 'Oh, I see. Perhaps it's not all to do with money.'

'Please tell me what's going on?'

He munched his toast thoughtfully and finally said, 'It's a silly fabrication – you should have been told. It's not as though you're a guest here. I'm surprised Hammond hasn't spilled the beans.'

'Which particular beans?'

'Viv and Hammond are related by marriage – not blood.'

I was thoroughly confused. 'Who's married? And to whom?'

'Each other, you little fool, each other. They're husband and wife.'

This information was so disorientating I couldn't put it together straight away. Now, of course, it's all fallen into place. Why Mr Brooke is always so irritable when I ask about Vivian. Why there seemed to be a Vivian-sized gap in every story. Given Mr Brooke's ambivalence, I wonder why on earth he is upholding this pretence – and how long it's gone on?

'You should get upstairs and pack before she gets back,' said Jonathan, pouring a cup of tea. 'She's always in a filthy mood after speaking to him.'

'I can't imagine it could get any filthier than just now.'

'Oh, that's where you're quite wrong. Here,' he said handing me the cup of tea. 'Take this with you.'

So here I am, in my room, packing haphazardly, my thoughts

flying off in a dozen directions. How can this happen now after last night? What will I do about William? I'm certainly not leaving without saying my goodbyes to Mr Brooke. Where will I go? I shall insist on her buying me an air ticket back to London. Although that would be horribly expensive and I'm not sure I could bear to fly – let alone such a distance – and also I just remembered that a flight destined for Nice crashed in the Alps a few years ago. Perhaps I will take the train after all.

Just now, as I was agonising over my exit plan, there was a knock on my door. I opened it to find Vivian, an unconvincing smile pasted on her face.

'Iris,' she began in an earnest voice. 'Please forgive me. I don't know how to explain my behaviour, except to say that I misunderstood the situation. Mr Brooke has explained it all to me and I am satisfied there has been no impropriety.' She glanced over my shoulder at my packing efforts. 'Please disregard everything I said. He is expecting you for work.'

I gave her the coldest look I have ever given another living creature – ironically I learned this from her. Impropriety! The cheek of her! One minute she's cavorting naked on the kitchen table, the next she's suspecting me of having some sort of intrigue with her husband, having dishonestly represented him as her brother. For a fleeting moment it occurred to me to wonder if he was actually blind – is that a ruse too? I am starting to go a little mad.

'I'm not entirely sure I want to stay,' I heard myself say. 'I need to give the matter some thought. But if I do decide to continue here I expect to be treated with respect, as should any employee.'

I could hardly believe these words were inserting themselves so grandly between us. My thoughts beautifully articulated, my tone firm and courteous but commanding too.

She looked as though she wanted to strangle me but squeezed out another humbled apology. Instead of my normal flustered response to the embarrassment caused by an apology that would incite me to counter-apologise, I continued in the same lofty tone. 'It's been revealed to me that Mr Brooke is in fact your husband – not your brother. Is that true?'

Vivian gave me her blank gaze of disbelief. 'Iris, I understand you've been doing a wonderful job getting the family business sorted out. We're really terribly grateful. Hammond is very appreciative and speaks highly of you.' She paused, no doubt hoping I would be distracted by a few sweet crumbs thrown in my path. 'Yes, he is my legal husband, however we haven't lived as man and wife for many years. The reason for the subterfuge is, as much as anything, to avoid gossip. People around here are very conservative about such things – traditional, let's say. Hammond and I are bound together by circumstances, not by choice. I would just ask that you protect our privacy. If not for me, then for him.'

She sounded genuine and for once I believed her. This was a different side of Vivian, one I haven't seen before and, let's face it, I have seen her from a variety of angles.

Mr Brooke made no mention of Vivian's visit; he was simply keen to move on with the work of notating and packing up all the raw materials. One slightly curious thing – despite his initial excitement about the rose harvest, when I asked when the rose absolute would arrive, he was evasive, dismissive even. I wonder if something has gone wrong there?

Later in the day, as I was packing up, he said, 'Vivian tells me you two are getting on well.'

I wasn't sure whether he was making this up for his own reasons or it was one of Vivian's machinations – which seemed the most likely – but I wanted no part of it. 'Mr Brooke, I'm sorry, but that is an outright lie. She is barely civil to me and sometimes extremely uncivil.'

'On what basis?'

'My assessment is that she needs me and resents me in equal measures.'

He gave a grunt of agreement.

'I understand that Vivian is your wife,' I said.

'She volunteered that?'

'No, Jonathan did. But she confirmed it.'

Mr Brooke laughed. 'That fool couldn't keep a secret to save his life.'

I wasn't amused. I felt owed some sort of explanation for this deception and he conceded reluctantly. 'We don't see eye-to-eye on most matters but, because of my situation, I'm obviously dependent on her to some degree. The property and business belong to my family and therefore Vivian needs me – preferably alive. Dead, it gets much more complicated.'

He said no more on that topic but asked if we could walk for a while and clear our heads. It is so companionable to wander along arm-in-arm with him now. The most pleasant path crosses the road and meanders down a winding lane into some woods beyond. The woods are scrappy compared to those of England – mostly pines – but for the sighted there are glimpses across to the sea. Sometimes he asks me to describe the scene, which I do to the best of my ability but my descriptions fall very short of the blue shimmering reality. I am now sadly aware that he doesn't even have the dimension of smell. The sensual nectar of wild jasmine, the bracing tang of pines after rain and the warm salt of the distant sea were mine alone.

Today, as we walked, he began to talk more about the Villa Rousseau and revealed that the property had been occupied by the Gestapo during the war. I asked where he lived during that time.

'Before the war I lived in the villa with my grandparents. As I'm sure you know, early in the war the South was in the Free Zone. Later we were occupied by the Italians, who were no bother but then, of course, they swapped sides. Once we had German masters, everything changed dramatically. When the Gestapo came and took our property, my grandparents went to our family in Menton. I moved to a small apartment above the factory.'

'The factory continued to operate?'

'To some degree,' he said. 'We all make compromises in wartime.'

So, for him at least, it was business as usual during the war. I know from the bills of lading that the raw ingredients had come from all corners of the earth. It is difficult to imagine how the factory could continue to operate without the aid of the Gestapo.

'It was around then I realised something was wrong with my sight,' he said. 'I knew my time was limited. From then it was a gradual decline, almost imperceptible at first but accumulative over the last decade. In some ways I'm fortunate – even a world of shadows is better than complete darkness.'

Thinking about this now, I am fairly sure *Aurélie* made its debut in the late 1940s. Allowing time for development, one could assume that he created it toward the end of the war, already knowing it would be his last composition. His final symphony.

Chapter Ten

An aerogramme came in the mail for me today. My immediate hope was that it was from Alan, reassuring me it was all a terrible mistake. I opened it, longing to hear his comforting voice apologising for the misunderstanding but my hopes were dashed when I realised that the handwriting was actually Ruth's.

Using every inch of the page, she lauded my brother's career ambitions, emphasised how important it was to create the right image and how vital that they move to a better house and mix with a different class of person. The future of my niece and nephew relied on the schools they attended and classmates they cultivated. Their future was dependent on funds from the sale of Linnet Lane. According to Ruth, my lack of cooperation stemmed from jealousy at my brother's standing in the world. I have (apparently) achieved nothing because of my wilful determination to be independent. I live only for myself. Now my selfish behaviour was preventing her family achieving their best. She was appealing to my better side. If that didn't work, they would proceed to court to challenge Father's will. She closed by

AMANDA HAMPSON

explaining that she was writing this letter of her own volition and she would appreciate my respecting its confidentiality.

Once again I'm being put upon to protect someone's little secret, which presents me with a quandary. Is it fair to reveal information and then demand confidentiality? It's as though Ruth has struck a blow and then insisted I protect her from reprimand. I believe that I have the right to refuse. In that light, I addressed an envelope to Mr Hubert and penned a quick note confirming that I wished to proceed in defending my father's will, should it come to that. I enclosed Ruth's poison-pen letter and sealed the envelope before I lost my nerve.

This afternoon there was a note on the hall table to say that William Beaumont had called and would phone again later in the evening. A postscript from Vivian noted that she was not my secretary and in future would not be accepting my personal calls. Despite that, I felt the most delicious tingling all over my body. The day had been hot, especially so as we are still working in that stuffy back bedroom of the cottage. I usually have my bath before dinner but settled for a quick flannel wash, not wanting to miss his call.

Rather than retire to my room immediately after dinner, I decided to bide my time in the drawing room and found myself rehearsing and editing our forthcoming conversation in my head. While I had found him attractive from the outset, there was nothing to indicate his interest in me until that moment when I became the object of his affections. I don't want to invest too much in this but he has never strayed far from my mind since that night.

I pottered about the bookshelves, thinking I might dabble in recent French history so I can discuss it more intelligently with Mr Brooke. My knowledge of the whole occupation business is all a little vague now.

The doors to the terrace were wide open and the sounds of cicadas shrilled in the warm night air. Jonathan had pulled an armchair into the doorway to catch a breeze. He cradled a brandy glass, his feet resting on one of Vivian's antique occasional tables. Geraldson has been away this week and, with Farley permanently indisposed, Jonathan has lost his late-night playmates and any distraction from steady drinking. He begged me to join him, extolling the virtues of a late-night snifter and singing the praises of the balmy night air.

'What is it you're looking for, girl?' He twisted around irritably in his chair and snorted at my explanation. 'They're short on facts in this house. It's all fabrications. Fantastical allusions, or is it delusions?' He lost his thread for a moment and found it again. 'They make it up as they go along. Improvise. Whatever suits on the day.'

I went over and sat down near him. He gave me a pitiful look. 'You're the only good . . . honest . . . wholesome . . . creature.' Tears coursed down his raddled cheeks.

While I would never actively desire Vivian's presence in a room, it would have been useful at that point. She does know how to handle him. I gave him my clean hankie. The pervading smell around Jonathan is of something dusty and forgotten, perhaps like a box of old love letters – a repository of dead dreams and lost hopes.

Dabbing at his eyes, he pressed my handkerchief to his nose, inhaled and gave a ragged sigh. 'Ask me anything. I have . . . the facts . . . at my fingertips.' He located these and wiggled them as evidence.

'Why do you stay here if you're so unhappy?' I asked.

'The answer is, I am more unhappy elsewhere. That is to say less happy. I'm at my *un*happiest away from Vivian and slightly less miserable with her. Unhappiness follows me everywhere I go, sniffing at my heels. Inescapable.'

'But don't you have a wife back in England?'

'Ex-wife by now, I expect. Ex-wives plural. All three paled by comparison to *her*. You see, I told you. I am the only one capable of delivering the facts, telling the honest unadorned truth of the matter.'

'And I appreciate your candour.' I smiled, attempting to lighten the mood.

'I had her once, you know,' he said, a creamy gaze softening his features. 'When I was young and lovely . . . in a field of buttercups . . . she wore a white cotton frock . . .'

This sounded rather whimsical to me, more like something he had seen in a film. Vivian has a knack of walking in on this sort of moment but fortunately she missed her cue because things then got much worse.

'She's *screwing* the kraut. She thinks no one knows.' He gave a bitter laugh and watched for my reaction over the rim of his brandy glass. 'You don't seem surprised. She's frightfully indiscreet. Anyway, don't go tattling to your chum – he might use it against her.'

'If the "kraut" you're referring to is Mr Geraldson, I thought he was a chum of yours?'

'Hardly. I tolerate him. With a measure of charm. I would prefer to challenge him to a duel at dawn. Pistols. Perhaps not dawn, more around mid-morning, when I'm at my peak.' He drained his glass and sunk further into his armchair.

'What line of work is Mr Geraldson in, do you know?'

'More British than the British, eh? Ever wondered why?' He stared gloomily into the night. 'He's in a trade of some sort. No, he's ah . . . God, what did Viv say? A broker of some sort. Not stocks, something else. Businesses.'

'Is he working for Vivian?' I was now keeping a very sharp eye on the door in case she appeared.

'She doesn't tell me much. Most likely. He's a wheeler-dealer I think. Here, don't say anything to Viv about our little conversation. What do you want to know all this for?'

'Just curious,' I said, standing up. 'It's late, I should go to bed.'

'Are you in love with him?'

'Who?'

'The Nose.'

'Mr Brooke? No, of course not —'

'Because he's old and tired and angry, like me?'

'Not at all. I hold him in very high esteem —'

He sat up, angry and surprisingly alert. 'Do you now? You don't know a damn thing about him. That bastard has more secrets than all of us put together. Not quite British, not quite French. Not quite married. Not quite divorced. Not quite sighted or completely blind for that matter. Sees what he wants to. He's . . . he's . . . like an emperor, toppled from his throne, living in a pleasantly scented exile, loyal to nothing but his art. Ask him what he did in the war. In fact, next time you have your pretty little nose in that dictionary, look up the word *passeur*. Might change your view somewhat. I'll save you the bother – he was a people-smuggler. Not to be trusted.' He lifted my hankie to his face, inhaled and closed his eyes. 'Extraordinary,' he sighed.

Drained of vitriol, he drifted off into a snoring slumber. As I got up to leave an acrid smell filled the air and a dark stain crept across the front of his trousers. The air was dense with lonely disappointment.

No word from William. I had almost forgotten about him – but not quite.

There's something mysterious going on at the cottage that will no doubt soon be causing a storm – one I do not want to get caught in. Over the past few weeks I have documented hundreds of Mr Brooke's little bottles and packed them in straw in small crates. In order to be thorough, I took it upon myself to number the crates and keep note in the ledger, cross-referenced to the contents. As instructed, I have been putting the packed crates into the storeroom beside the cottage but I now realise that the crates are gradually disappearing. Someone is spiriting them away in the night.

It's possible Vivian's involved – clearly she's the one who wants this done. But if that were the case, why the secrecy? Or am I the only one who hasn't been told? The other possibility is that Mr Brooke – perhaps with the help of Monsieur Lapointe – is removing the crates to another location. It would be helpful to know who and why, preferably before the other party finds out. I am torn as to whether to bring it up or not.

Postscript for today: William telephoned this evening and has invited me out for supper on Friday!

After three weeks away, Mrs Somerville arrived back at the villa this afternoon like a weary old soldier. She greeted me warmly but I could tell by Vivian's vexed expression that her reappearance was unexpected.

The minute Mrs S went up to her room, Vivian turned to me and said crossly, 'Not a word until this morning. There was talk of them going to New York on the Queen Mary after the funeral. I naturally thought — Blast! I've made a mess of this! The sisters arrive at the end of the month, and now I'll be a room short. Where's Didier gone?' Without waiting for a response she stamped off, slamming doors all the way to her office.

Mrs Somerville came down to supper this evening tastefully bejewelled and upholstered in a green satin sheath she picked up in Paris. Contrary to her previously poor opinion of the British, as a result of her hobnobbing she seems to have acquired more respect. 'Jessie's family owns a huge spread,' she told us. 'Entire villages, enormous great house, stables of horses. But not a luxury in sight. Threadbare rugs. Not even electric heating. And the draughts through the place in the middle of summer – imagine winter! You'd have to sleep in your furs. Quite an eye-opener for a pampered Yank, believe me!'

'I expect they'll lash out on some draught excluders with Farley's money,' said Jonathan.

'The funeral was all very awkward,' continued Mrs Somerville. 'I got the impression people were just making an appearance. No love lost for the guy, that's for sure. Turns out he has a son from his previous marriage but Jessie will get a few bucks out of it.'

'She's fortunate the deceased was British,' said Jonathan. 'In France the children are the protected heirs by law – not the wife. Regardless of the will, the son would automatically get half the estate, the wife only a quarter, perhaps less if there were a number of children.'

'Poor *maman* raises the ungrateful little wretches only to have them steal her home out from under her,' said Vivian.

'And what about the other quarter?' I asked.

'It's termed *quotité disponible*. In other words, you can leave it to whomever you wish,' said Vivian. 'The dogs' home, for example.'

'Fortunately I have none of those problems,' said Mrs S. 'My money is my own. I made every cent through my own labours and no one can take that away from me.'

'Let me guess,' said Jonathan playfully. 'You're an oil tycoon. No? A . . . beet farmer. Oh, I have it – a madam!'

Vivian frowned at him but Mrs Somerville responded with a screech of laughter. '*Brassieres!* I had a little dress shop and top-heavy women often came in looking for a good comfortable brassiere. So I sat down and designed a little something and then I found out how to manufacture them. And *pouf!* They flew out the door. Somerville Brassieres: you've probably heard of them. It's a huge business now, too big for me. My two sons run it all.'

Vivian no doubt considers the whole endeavour vulgar but I found myself smiling at this wonderful tale. After dinner, I sat with Mrs S in the garden and we chatted a little and gazed at the stars together. On her own she is less bumptious and I wonder if she feels the need to put on a show. Perhaps someone told her that one needs to be controversial and entertaining when one dines with company in France.

'I can confide in you, honey,' she told me. 'You've never been anything other than sweet with everyone. You'd think butter wouldn't melt in Lady Jessie's mouth, but I was chewed up and spat out by that girl.'

'In what way?' I asked.

'Well, once we arrived in Paris, she started to misbehave. Badly. Drinking far too much wine at dinner, as she did here, but so much more embarrassing in a high-class restaurant. Picking arguments with me about every little thing – three miserable days.'

'But you still went back to England with her?'

'I felt obliged, with her being recently widowed. I'd been in touch with the family. I couldn't just dump her. Besides, she didn't seem to be at all aware of how upsetting her behaviour was to me. Her family were extremely courteous and made me very welcome, but all the same . . .'

'I'm sorry you had to go through all that. She seemed so fond of you.'

'I thought so too. I loved her like a daughter,' she said almost tearfully. 'Actually, now I'm relieved she's not my kin. She's a real handful. The family are eccentric and crazy indulgent about her wacky behaviour. Tantrums – oh my lord!'

'Maybe they feel guilty about trading her off to Farley?'

'I've thought about that. I don't believe that was true any more. Or probably anything she said about his . . . predilections. Who knows, maybe he was after his conjugal rights.' We both shuddered at the thought. 'Actually, I wouldn't put it past the little minx to have drugged herself.'

Oh strange and wondrous night! I will start at the beginning and savour every moment.

William collected me in his smart grey Wolseley and we motored up to Valbonne, a small village perched on the steep hills above the Côte d'Azur. Our conversation was a little forced at first. We asked each other questions, answering them meticulously as though being interviewed. There were missteps as we rushed to fill silences and then apologised, urging the other to go first. After a time, our unease became a source of humour and we found ourselves more relaxed and casual with each other.

On the walk from the car to the restaurant, he offered me his arm in a most chivalrous manner. I felt quite the part in a cream dress with matching bolero jacket, compliments of Lady J's trunk. We wandered the cobblestoned streets looking for all the world like a genuine couple, which I confess to have thoroughly enjoyed. I felt excited and fluttery in his presence but not really nervous – quite natural and content. Everything seemed so vivid and I felt alive to all that was about me.

He had booked a table in a restaurant in the main square. We were to dine *en plein air* under a clear starry sky. Although William is quietly spoken and reserved in his ways, when the waiter came to our table he discussed the menu and asked questions confidently in enviably fluid French. The waiter treated him with due respect, or less scorn than one comes to expect, and William consolidated their relationship by ordering on the fellow's recommendations.

Out of duty I asked after Topsy and Sebastian and he said they were fine; he had seen them earlier in the week. 'Do you often go to Le Negresco?' I asked. 'It's terribly posh.'

'Occasionally. Topsy likes it there. She craves the society of the types who inhabit the place. I don't really care for those sorts myself.' He glanced at me quickly. 'You know I'm not referring to you.'

I laughed. 'I don't see myself as inhabiting the place, just passing through.'

He toyed with his napkin, flipping it back and forth. 'You should know I'm not wealthy like Sebastian. I'm from the poor side of the family. Our mothers are sisters; his fortune comes from his father's family. I'm just a bean counter for an accountancy firm in London.'

'Oh, I thought you lived here.'

'I do. We have a number of important clients here on the Riviera. As I speak French, I was given the opportunity to come out and open a branch office about two years ago.' He explained it was a small operation, just him and a secretary. Over dinner, he regaled me with amusing stories about his adventures with fabulously wealthy and eccentric clients. Isolated by wealth and mistrust, they enlist his services for all sorts of purchases and investments, from spending exorbitant sums on luxury yachts to investing millions in the Middle East. It's easy to imagine him being very sensible and down-to-earth, making sure all is in order. He radiates dependability and good intention but there is something else more complex; I picked up strains of uncertainty – self-doubt, maybe? I often intuit the scent of crushed violets around him, as though something were grinding him down.

'If you get it right for them, clients are prone to buying extravagant gifts,' he said. 'Even for their humble accountant.'

I expected him to show me a watch or some cufflinks but it seems his Wolseley was a gift from a client. I wondered if his bosses in London knew the scale of their clients' generosity, but thought better of mentioning it.

'When we met at Le Negresco, there was some intrigue about your employer – the perfume fellow?'

'It's not really an intrigue. Topsy was making more of it than necessary,' I said. 'He's something of a recluse and part of my job is to protect his privacy.'

'Like a bodyguard?'

'I suppose so,' I laughed.

'Topsy is very eager to meet him for some odd reason.'

I felt a twinge of concern that must have shown on my face.

'Don't worry, I'm not here as Topsy's lackey,' he assured me.

'No, of course not, I didn't think —'

He placed his hand gently over mine. 'Let's not talk about Topsy or Sebastian tonight.'

There was no further mention of Mr Brooke and we found many other things to talk about. We discovered we both enjoyed walking and shared a love of the Lake District in particular. He is extremely well-read and, of course, much more widely travelled than myself. Before we knew it, the evening had disappeared. After dinner we wandered arm-in-arm through the darkened lanes. There was a blissful sense of intimacy between us and we stopped on several occasions to exchange lingering kisses. It was as though time stretched into the distance and the world was held at bay. There was only this moment, this night redolent with honeysuckle – the scent of contentment.

Chapter Eleven

It is almost a week since that evening with William. I have found it difficult to think of anything else, reliving every gentle kiss and caress. I do hope to hear from him soon.

Mr Brooke has been increasingly unwell. There is the most appalling foul odour in the cottage as though everything has become rancid and rotten. From deep within that overwhelming stench there is a pervading smell of utter despair. He has been confined to his bed, so no work can take place. Two days ago he simply shouted at me to get out, which I did without further ado. Now he's been admitted to a hospital in Marseille for a few days.

While he was away, Menna must have opened up the place and ventilated it because when I went to the cottage today the odour was much diminished. Although he won't discuss it with me at all, whatever is going on with his health is clearly not over. In the past few weeks, the doctor has been to the cottage almost every day — as has Father Furolo. The three of them spend hours sitting in the garden talking and even at a distance I have picked up sharp traces of dissension.

After many delays, we finally completed the inventory this morning and packed the last of the materials away. Although Mr Brooke was obviously exhausted, I felt duty-bound to raise the issue of the disappearing crates.

'That's not possible! Are you absolutely certain? Go and have another look. Jesus Christ! They better not be gone! What are you waiting for?'

I went out and checked even though I didn't need to. I knew the number of crates had diminished but discovered there are now only a few left with no attempt being made to disguise the losses. I reported back only to be told furiously I could go. He had a call to make.

So, safe to assume that Vivian is behind this. Now all the materials have been packed, I realised it was quite likely that the last of the crates will be removed this evening.

Once the house was asleep, I positioned myself at the upstairs hallway window which provides a view across the orchard to the cottage. Menna returned from her nightly chores with Mr Brooke and disappeared into her room, which I have discovered is in the cellar. Before long, two figures appeared on the downstairs patio and went off into the orchard.

I slipped down the back stair and waited in the shadow of the house near the cellar stairs. Menna must have recognised my shoes as I passed her window because she came out and beckoned me into her room. I couldn't make out much in the darkness.

Being half underground, the barred window is set high enough that you need a stool to see anything other than sky. She fetched a box for me to stand on and we stood side by side, watching out the window.

Vivian arrived and unlocked the potting shed, then Geraldson appeared out of the gloom carrying the last three crates. They both went inside and we could see the flashing of a torch as they rearranged the contents of the packed shed. Eventually they came out and locked up. After a brief discussion, Vivian went back into the house but Geraldson headed straight toward the cellar. Moments later, there was a thump on Menna's door. I huddled in the corner of the room, out of sight. Geraldson spoke brusquely. Someone would arrive *ce soir* – tonight. It was all a bit of a jumble but I thought he was telling her not to go to sleep – *ne va pas dormir*. I then caught the word *clé* – key.

Once we were certain he had gone, we made our way out to the shed. Menna unlocked the door and we slipped inside and closed it behind us. By the light of Menna's candle we took in the sight of two dozen crates, boxes and tins – everything from the storeroom. We walked back to Menna's room and sat down at her little table. The candlelight flattered the grim little room, really more of a cell, with a few sticks of furniture and an army cot against one wall. Cold damp air. Winter must be appalling. Disgraceful she should have to live in these conditions.

Although communication is frustratingly difficult, I could see in her face that we shared a sense of finality. Tonight was the end of something after which everything would change. There was a tacit agreement that I would stay for the collection of the crates. Menna made sweet mint tea on a gas ring. She brought a pack of Spanish playing cards to the table and we spent the next couple of hours keeping lookout and, ironically, playing double patience.

At around 1 a.m. we heard the sound of a van approach. It stopped near the villa and the engine was turned off. Menna blew out the candle and we took up our post at the window. We could make out the figure of a man, short and stocky, walking up the path to the shed. He stopped at the door, rattled the padlock and glanced around. His face was illuminated for a second in the flare of a match as he lit his cigarette.

I heard a sharp intake of breath beside me. '*Ah non – le Corse!*' So soft it could have been imagined, but there was no mistaking Menna's fear, that pungent metallic odour like blood. She rushed over to the cot, dropped to her knees and pulled something out from under it. I caught the glint of a blade as she concealed it in the folds of her skirt and then slipped out the door.

I watched with trepidation from the window as Menna approached the shed, unlocked it and opened both doors wide. The man flashed his torchlight over the crates and flicked the beam onto Menna's face. Unflinching, she made no effort to cover her eyes. This seemed to gall him because he took a step toward her and prodded her in the chest with his torch. She turned away, picked up a crate and carried it down the path toward where his van was parked. He sat down on one of the boxes and smoked as she walked back and forth with the goods. The terrifying stench of a brutal man, a predator, was putrid in the night air.

Eventually I saw him flash his torch around the empty shed. The only crate that remained was the one he sat on. He stood up; there was a splash of embers as he flicked his cigarette into the garden. He closed one of the doors, left the other half open

and waited for Menna to return. There was a sense of him read-
ying himself. He fumbled with his clothing and I presumed he
planned to urinate in the garden. But he was removing his belt.
Waiting for Menna. The trap was set. I didn't know what to do.
I looked around for something to use against him but it was
so dark in the room I could barely see the floor beneath me.
I opened the door and crept up the cellar steps, crouched near
the top and watched. Perhaps I could at least distract him so
Menna could escape. Where was she?

It took him a while to realise he had been outwitted and that
Menna was not coming back for that final crate. She had vanished into the night. Finally, he picked it up himself and stamped
off down the path. I didn't breathe easy until I heard the sound
of his van recede into the distance. Menna then came running
down the cellar steps. We clasped each other's hands and tried to
smother our relieved laughter.

Mr Brooke's shoulders slumped in defeat when I told him what I
had witnessed last night. He asked if I had seen the man before.
I repeated what Menna had said. Curiously, he made no comment
about the fact that Menna had spoken. 'That bloody Corsican
thug. So that's it – gone. Vivian got the jump on me.'

'Do you know where to?'

'Geneva, so I believe. Apparently Geraldson's brokered some
deal with a pharmaceutical firm; chemists who think they can
make perfume.'

'Can't you stop it?'

'What can I do? It really doesn't matter any more. Those
materials are replaceable. It's all coming to an end anyway. Vivian

has no vision for the future. She's only looking to resolve her current crisis.'

'Which is?'

'Same as always – money. More money. She can have this battle. It's the war that I care about. *That* I will not lose.'

'What about the formulas – don't they need those?'

He gave an ironic shrug. 'That's what they need now. I'm assured it is all just chemistry. Like filling in a prescription, more or less. So that is what we will give them. Tomorrow I'll dictate the formulations to you. Let her know. Might calm her down.'

I saw Vivian prior to dinner and passed on the news, expecting a warm response. She looked suspicious. 'How clever of you. Hammond said this himself, did he? It's not like him to announce he will cooperate. Generally he either does or he doesn't.'

'Is he very ill?' I asked. 'He won't discuss it.'

'Well, that's his prerogative, isn't it?' She obviously remembered that she was making a conscious effort to be pleasant to me now the finish line is in sight because she then softened her tone. 'He may well have to go into hospital for an operation in the next several weeks. But once this final job is done, your role with him will be finished. You're no doubt desperate to get home to London by now.' She gestured toward the dining-room door. 'Let us join the others, shall we?'

Although the conversation unsettled me, I had to force a smile as we were joined this evening by the fabled sisters from Florida; a couple of dry old sticks with brittle perms and straying lipstick, so angular their clothes hang off them as if draped on coathangers. They smell rather artificial to me, like this 'air freshener' that is all the craze now. As they both answer to Miss Anderson, they insisted we address them as Shirley and Lillian.

Mrs Somerville is clearly delighted that numbers from her side of the Atlantic are building and did her best to establish a rapport with them.

While the rest of the table was distracted by the newcomers, I noticed Vivian catch Geraldson's eye and give him a nod. He glanced at me, raised his eyebrows in pleasant surprise and tipped his glass in an almost imperceptible tribute.

It has been evident in recent weeks that Vivian has received an injection of funds. Normally something of a miser, she watches every centime like a hawk and won't hear of anything being sent to town for repair. But during the lead-up to the arrival of the sisters, the house has teemed with tradesmen and a sixth bedroom has been renovated, leaving only two remaining in their dilapidated state.

Passing the new room each day, I had watched the transformation with admiration. There is no doubt Vivian knows what she is doing in this regard. She has impeccable taste for the style of *décor* favoured by wealthy visitors to the continent, which could be described as a sort of timeless French luxuriousness – Marie Antoinette tailored to the well-heeled tourist. She ran the project with military precision from the frenzied preparations – stripping wallpaper and paint and sanding floors – to the refurbishment – walls repapered, floors polished, curtains hung, rugs laid. An extravagant crystal chandelier arrived from Italy and was installed by four men with much fuss and bother and furious swearing. French antique furniture was put into place under her precise direction: a four-poster bed, ornate writing desk, armchairs, mirrors and paintings. The villa is not blessed with a bathroom for every bedroom (quite normal for a family home), but Vivian has created these using the smaller bedrooms and storage areas. Overall it must have cost her a pretty penny – tens of thousands of francs, one suspects. Although they are apparently here for three months, it is hard to imagine that the tariff the sisters will pay would come close to meeting the cost of the renovation. Although I suppose there is always the chance they will return or recommend the place to other members of the tribe of wealthy, bored women on an endless Grand Tour of Europe.

Lillian and Shirley have quickly established an unwavering routine that is probably unaltered wherever they go. They have hired a limousine and driver and leave the villa after dinner every night for casinos in either Cannes, Nice or Monte Carlo. They arrive home sometime in the early hours and sleep until noon, when they arise and paste themselves to sun chairs, toasting their desiccated skin and painting their nails until it is once more time to don their diamonds, have a bite to eat and head out into the night. The first evening they were quite congenial, but now they have a terribly rude habit of only talking to each other, as though they are in a restaurant rather than at a communal dining table.

We are such an odd assortment, conversation can be a strain at the best of times. The London papers arrive once a week and Jonathan reads every word, so that provides a basis for conversation under a mandate of neutrality, which we now all adhere to – even Mrs Somerville – as dissension makes for poor digestion. Generally Vivian and Jonathan hold things together, although Geraldson has become more relaxed and at least makes some effort these days. He too is very well-informed about international affairs but exceedingly diplomatic. Mrs Somerville is less controversial – obviously Farley had ruffled her feathers with his reactionary views. Provided I have something worthwhile to offer, I make my small contribution. We have evolved into a conversational quintet that had, with practice, become relatively harmonious. But now we have this discordant duo in our midst, it all feels rather artificial.

Mrs Somerville has been attempting to ingratiate herself with the sisters since their arrival, with limited success. Why she bothers, I don't know. They are so uninteresting and uninterested in the rest of us. Since her return, Mrs Somerville seemed to have forgotten all about her ambitions to meet Mr Brooke. However, at dinner this evening, in a desperate bid to gain their attention, she turned to the sisters and announced, 'It's all very hush-hush but there's a famous perfumer living right here on the estate. I'm hoping that Miss Brooke is going to introduce him one day soon. I, for one, would be just fascinated to meet him.'

'It is out of the question,' said Vivian, glaring at me. 'He's very busy and not at all well. He's only recently been released from hospital.'

'Oh, I'm so sorry to hear that. Is it something serious?' Mrs Somerville's curiosity was piqued.

'We're waiting to see if this latest treatment has worked,' said Vivian.

Impervious to the note of finality indicating the closure of that topic, Mrs Somerville wedged her foot in. 'What sort of treatment is he undergoing? I have an excellent physician in Paris, I could —'

'Really, thank you, but it's all in hand,' Vivian assured her.

The rising tension at the table was beginning to make everyone squirm but Mrs S didn't seem to know how to extricate herself. 'I just thought —'

'Maggots,' said Jonathan fiercely.

Vivian pursed her lips, disapproving, but said nothing.

Mrs Somerville's lips twisted in a knot of disgust. The Anderson sisters were suddenly all ears. I felt quite sick. How absolutely appalling!

'You insisted on knowing. I'm telling you. He's been undergoing maggot treatment.'

'I didn't mean to pry. I was trying to help. I don't know what maggot treatment is,' said Mrs Somerville. 'Do you mean real maggots?'

Jonathan was turning puce, thoroughly rattled by this intrusive display of bad manners. Vivian leaned over and patted his hand to calm him. 'Mr Brooke is diabetic,' she explained. 'He is suffering from gangrene and this treatment is considered preferable to amputation.' She held Mrs Somerville's eye with her magisterial gaze. 'Now, can we please change the subject? This is hardly a suitable topic for the dinner table.' And, for once, there was a sense of universal agreement.

It seems as though Mr Brooke is being systematically stripped of everything he has and everything he is. The thought of the maggots makes me feel ill every time I think of it. On no account would I ever raise that one with him. We were supposed to start documenting the formulas a week ago but he has been too unwell, so today was the first opportunity. He would, he told me, be dictating the formulas from memory. There's something queer about this. 'Surely they were recorded somewhere?' I asked.

He agreed there had been a journal. 'Probably one of the most valuable books of fragrance formulas in the world. It had the formulations my grandfather created, my mother's and some of mine. It was lost during the war. What Vivian has sold off is the scraps that are left of the business. She obviously can't sell the name of Rousseau, only the perfume brands. What I'm going to give you are the more recent formulas, the ones I keep in my head.'

'What about *Aurélie*?'

'What about her?' he snapped. The 'her' hung in the air between us; I had caught him off guard.

'Will you give them the formula for *Aurélie*?'

'That formulation has been lost. Destroyed. Let's get this over with.'

I opened up the doors and windows to allow the bright day outside to peek into the room. Early in the day the garden is at its very best, dewy bright, refreshed by the sprinklers overnight. By late afternoon there is a dusty weariness in the atmosphere.

I set up the typewriter on a small table near him so he could be comfortable in his armchair. Like a poet drumming up stanzas, he dictated the formulas to me and I typed them up. Initially I was concerned about the accuracy of his memory, then I began to suspect that the wily old devil was actually concocting the recipes as he went – literally throwing them off the scent. He began with all the Rousseau fragrances that are legitimate and well-known such *Clémence*, *Océane* and *Madame Beaulieu* – although I have my doubts as to whether they are accurate formulations. I think he believes they won't notice the small anomalies that would differentiate a pleasant scent from a work of art. He then began to pad out the list with unfamiliar names – these had a more Germanic flavour, such as *Berengaria* and *Crimilda*. On the pretext of checking the spelling I looked up the meanings in his reference book of names. I quite see why these two stuck in his head. *Berengaria* means 'strong as a bear' and *Crimilda* 'she who wears a fighting helmet'! Where on earth was he getting these from? Finally he wore out his repertoire of German female names and dictated a formula for *Eine kleine Nachtmusik* (rather amusing) followed by *Schadenfreude* and I burst out laughing. He feigned bewilderment but then a sly smile crept in. 'Am I going too far?'

'If you want them to believe you – yes!'

'All right. Some of the older fragrances, such as *Clémence*, are somewhat dated, they can have those . . .' he trailed off and I realised he didn't have a complete plan.

'In trying to keep them happy, you're going to make them suspicious.'

'I'm not trying to keep them happy, I'm trying to keep them busy!'

And so, with the help of the reference book, we put our heads together and retitled the fragrances with more evocative French names such as *Aimée, Sabine* and *Nathalie*. Clearly he is trying to bulk up his repertoire so that it will take them possibly years to fine-tune the discordant formulas he has provided. Then who is to say the recipes were wrong; that it's not the fault of the pharmacist?

As I was leaving this evening, he made the comment that I should keep this business about Menna's ability to speak to myself. Vivian was not aware of it.

'Do you know anything about her? Has she talked to you?'

'Nothing. She very sensibly only speaks when absolutely necessary. Doesn't ask nosy questions.'

'How long has she worked here?'

'I don't know, ten or twelve years,' he said.

'So during the war?'

'Look, none of this is anything to do with you. It's difficult to be an Algerian in France. For whatever reason, Menna decided that silence made life easier. Especially around Vivian.'

I told him I didn't understand what he meant by that. How could it be easier to have no voice? He brushed me off, as usual, telling me it was a complex situation, impossible for me as a foreigner to understand. And I should keep my nose out of other people's business. If I add that outburst to the other clues I have about Menna's situation, including the fact that Vivian hid her when the police came, my guess is that Menna is an illegal unpaid servant. A precarious situation, powerless and at Vivian's behest. Silence is both her weapon and her protection.

Chapter Twelve

Not a word from William. It has taken all my strength not to be heartbroken but I am horribly disappointed. I must have misunderstood what happened between us. What a fool I am.

Alexander has called (it seems that Vivian is still accepting calls for me), back in touch after a lengthy absence chasing around after Freddy. He was quite frank about his neglect of our friendship but plans to make it up to me by organising a picnic in honour of my birthday on Sunday. He has invited Topsy and Sebastian and I am hoping upon hope that William will also be there and I can get some sense of what has happened.

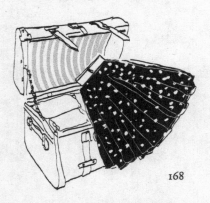

This morning dawned as a picnic-perfect day and I caught the bus down to Cannes to meet Alexander and Freddy. Deeper investigation of Lady Jessica's trunk revealed a pretty polka-dot skirt that fitted with my white blouse, plimsolls and a whisper of *Iridescence*.

Every time I thought of the possibly of seeing William my tummy went all jittery which, combined with the momentum of the bus roaring down the hills and swinging around the bends, left me quite queasy by the time I arrived in Cannes. I therefore wasn't entirely thrilled to discover that this was not a blanket-on-the-grass picnic with sandwiches and lemonade. We were taking a boat to Île Sainte-Marguerite, a small island off the coast of Cannes.

It was the full fiasco – Freddy in a captain's cap at the helm of a motor launch. Robertson, his surly manservant, was on board and in charge of hampers of food and buckets packed with ice and champagne. The ferry from Dover to Calais had been my first boating experience – this was my second – so Alexander had his work cut out to coax me onboard. But he and Freddy were so welcoming that, once plied with champagne, I was fine.

It was at least another half an hour before a limousine, chauffeur at the wheel, pulled up on the dock and three children tumbled out, a girl and two older boys, all aged between perhaps eight and twelve, followed by a uniformed nanny and Topsy and Sebastian. Disappointingly, no William.

They all piled onboard with great excitement and the nanny, who turned out to be a country girl from Cornwall, was run ragged by the wild children. The little girl immediately went into the cabin and emerged with an expensive brass telescope (which she dropped overboard before the day was out), the oldest boy entered into negotiations with Freddy to commandeer the steering wheel and, within minutes, the middle child had fallen overboard. Fortunately he was buoyant and Nanny was able to grab him by the scruff and haul him back on deck. Topsy and Sebastian, enjoying their champagne, were blithely unaware of the turmoil their children were causing onboard. I felt nothing but dismay at the thought of being trapped with this dreadful ensemble, first within the confines of a boat and then on an island. What a miserable birthday!

Just as we were about to cast off, the little girl – still in possession of the telescope at that point – said she could see Uncle William getting out of a taxi. The sun emerged from behind my gloomy cloud and I was now looking forward to the day ahead.

'William, darling, how lovely. So you haven't abandoned us entirely,' said Topsy as he came on board.

'Of course not.' He brushed a kiss on both her cheeks, shook hands with each of the men onboard and finally came to me. As his lips touched my cheek a spark of static electricity gave us both a jolt. 'Gosh! Sorry, Iris – I don't usually have that effect.' He gave a surprised laugh. Everyone was watching us now, especially Topsy.

'I expect it's some sort of nautical phenomenon,' I said, but could tell by his eyes that we both knew otherwise.

He accepted a glass of champagne and then another when the first was spilt by marauding children. Nanny, who was surprisingly adept at knots, managed to secure the children to each other and the railings with a length of rope. Freddy started the engines and we set off across the bay.

Once we disembarked, the island itself was highly agreeable, quiet and peaceful with woods of umbrella pines and eucalypts that gave off a wonderful invigorating odour. We all helped carry picnic blankets and folding sun chairs off the boat and settled under some pines that offered views across the bay to Cannes with a distant blue shadow of the mountains as its backdrop.

Robertson busied himself with wicker hampers of food, setting out a veritable banquet of baguettes, cold meats, chicken, sausage, lettuce, tomatoes and jellies and chocolate *gâteau* for a birthday dessert, as well as buckets of champagne and rosé. I had a quiet chuckle thinking back to picnics of my childhood. A flask of tea with egg and cress sandwiches wrapped in wax paper. Extra blankets in case it got cold, which it invariably did, and always – my father's pride and joy – a collapsible canvas windbreak that could be erected on any terrain. A far cry from this gentle paradise.

The children gnawed on legs of chicken and soon scattered to explore with Nanny in pursuit. Topsy and Sebastian may find their children amusing but Nanny does not appear to share that sentiment. She's probably already seeking less hectic employment with some nice quiet children content to gaze in wonder as she reads *Wind in the Willows* aloud to them.

Everyone seemed more relaxed once the children galloped off into the woods. Robertson retired to the boat to keep his own company and we stretched out on the blankets, dipping into the food and wine. Even Freddy was calm and amiable and only played a couple of quiet pieces on his violin that weren't too bad. Either he has been practising or his errors are less jarring in the open air, but whoever takes a Stradivarius on a picnic I don't know.

Alexander was happy and settled. He and Freddy are planning a trip to Morocco together. 'He's a delight when I get him away from the Riviera crowd,' Alexander told me quietly. 'Not as agitated. We have friends in Marrakech; we might rent a house and stay a few months.'

I told him that my days in the Riviera were also numbered as my post was coming to an end. Generous soul that he is, he immediately invited me to come and stay in Marrakech if I felt so inclined.

Sebastian has a writerly fascination for the history of Île Sainte-Marguerite and initiated a debate about the true identity of the man in the iron mask who was imprisoned in the fort for between ten, twenty or thirty years, depending on who you believe. Knowing nothing of the subject, I couldn't participate but enjoyed sneaking glances at William's regal profile as he put forward his considered theories. He has a twig-dry sense of humour and one has to stay alert for teasing and irony. I lay on the rug watching patches of sunlight as they played through the pines, listening to the sound of William's voice, and felt very contented.

I must have dozed off for a while because when I opened my eyes, everyone had wandered away apart from Topsy, who stayed behind to 'watch over me'. The blue sky had been replaced by banks of clouds and there was dampness in the air. I was stiff and cold, the wine sour in my mouth. Topsy fetched a large thermos from the hamper and poured me some coffee. 'You and William seem to be hitting it off,' she said, sitting down on the rug beside me. 'I wouldn't have thought he was your type, really. He can be a terrible flirt.'

Though groggy, I was immediately wary. Topsy shares one of Vivian's worst traits. You cannot depend on anything either of them says as being genuine. It's all inference, a way of prying designed to coax or provoke you into revelation. 'Really? I hadn't noticed that in him,' I said.

'It was actually Seb's idea that he ask you out to supper. He thinks William's lazy in that regard; doesn't put in the effort. He's becoming a confirmed bachelor. I was rather surprised you accepted.'

'It's not as though I have so many suitors I can turn men down,' I replied, attempting levity.

'No. I suppose not. I thought you were enamoured of your boss, the perfumer chap.'

I was so cross I nearly spilt my coffee. 'Not at all. I can't imagine why you would think such a thing. I care about him a great deal but have no romantic feelings for him whatsoever. If you met him you'd understand.'

She seemed heartened by the fact that I was rattled; she likes to have an effect. 'I want him to make me a perfume like yours,' she said. 'My own signature perfume. I don't care what it costs. I would have thought that would be a perfumer's dream. But you seem determined – rather selfishly, I might add – to keep him all to yourself.'

'It's nothing to do with me! He's blind and ill. He doesn't even have the means to make perfume any more. The business has been sold. Everything's gone.'

'Oh, that is unfortunate,' she said huffily, as though she were the only person disadvantaged by this turn of events. She stood up, brushed off her skirt and gave me a forgiving smile. 'Shall we take a walk? Robertson can tidy all this away and we'll have your cake on the boat.'

She offered her hands and pulled me to my feet; suddenly we were face-to-face, holding hands like square dancers. She tilted her pert little nose and gave a delicate sniff. Her eyes glossed over with tears. 'Iris, how can I become good like you? I hate myself for being such a cow.' Fortunately she didn't require an answer but linked arms with me affectionately and drew me down the path toward the woods to find the others.

By the time we found the rest of our party who had headed inland, large plops of rain started to fall. Everyone was shouting at once as we all ran helter-skelter along the winding paths through the woods. The rain pelted down. The children were in their element, their excitement infectious. We were all laughing at the chaos as we rushed down to the jetty and piled onto the boat. Robertson had packed up the picnic and sat smoking patiently as he watched the spectacle unravel before him.

We all squeezed into the tiny cabin and within minutes everyone was out of sorts. Topsy was furious that her shoes were ruined; Freddy equally distressed over his violin, understandably. Goodness knows what happened to the birthday *gâteau*. The children, cold and wet, took turns to squabble and cry. Dear William wrapped a rug around my shoulders but the wet squash below deck was too much for me. I went up and stood behind Robertson under the canopy as he navigated the choppy waters across the bay back to Cannes. Warm under my rug, buffeted by the wind and the weather, I felt quite restored, the sourness of that conversation with Topsy left behind on the island.

William came up on deck and stood close beside me, not quite touching as we watched the approaching shore. I can't imagine what he was thinking but I was clutching at every moment just being in his radius. As we pulled into the wharf, he turned to me and said, 'I'm sorry, Iris. I owe you an explanation.'

That was all. We didn't have another moment alone, so I have no idea what to expect or when to expect it. Or if he was simply stating a fact.

Now that my work is finished, Vivian would prefer I simply vanish. The sight of me seems to grate on her nerves. Conversely, Mr Brooke appears to be manufacturing reasons to retain me. I'm now dreading going home as I have been informed by Mr Hubert that Mr and Mrs Alan Turner will proceed to court to put Father's 'intention' to the test.

I have the sense that time is also slipping away for dear Mr Brooke. The hideous rotting smell is back and more dreadful than ever. He uses morphine against the pain which makes him a little tipsy. Disconcerting in itself. Jonathan revealed that Mr Brooke is due to be admitted to hospital again, this time to amputate his leg. He has made no mention of it but is obviously resistant to the whole procedure. It's all too horrible. He is clearly very unwell and anxious to have everything in the cottage sorted out. He had an art dealer come and remove all the paintings for auction; many of these belonged to his grandmother.

My role this last week has been to sort out hundreds of books and memorabilia from his travels, some to be packed up and stored – destination as yet unknown – and the rest destroyed. Every day we accumulate boxes full of papers he wants destroyed. Ideally the whole lot would go on a bonfire but he insists on it being done discreetly, so I've been laboriously burning them in the fireplace.

———

The disappearance of the scrawny sisters was today's drama. As a result of their habit of not appearing until luncheon, it wasn't apparent until late this afternoon that they had scarpered without settling their bill! In retrospect, there was something a little out of kilter at dinner last night; they had reverted to being the charming guests of the first evening, making far more effort than in the last couple of weeks.

My mind is obviously elsewhere because there were several other clues. Passing Shirley's room on the way to supper last night, the door was slightly ajar and I noticed the room was immaculately tidy. Most unlike previous glimpses when it looked like a careless child's bedroom with clothes draped everywhere and shoes scattered on the floor. As well, despite the balmy temperature, both sisters wore their minks out into the night. And that was the last we would see of them. It appears their driver and another man entered surreptitiously via the back stair and collected their trunks while we were all in the dining room. Makes one suspect they are quite practised at this sort of thing.

Vivian is absolutely furious. Understandably, given they not only did a bunk without paying but she poured thousands of francs into the refurbishment on the understanding they were here for at least three months. This is such a trusting British way to run a business, allowing guests to run up bills over weeks or months. It can't be the first time she's been caught out. I would hope that Jonathan pays month to month; he's apparently been here most of the year.

Geraldson departed a few days ago, presumably to deliver the formulations now all meticulously typed up. But on my way to my room this evening I noticed the Corsican – who, on closer inspection, looks like a nasty piece of work – leaving Vivian's office. The sisters may have a head start but their gambling habits will make them relatively easy to track down.

Probably as a result of the morphine, Mr Brooke is becoming a different person. On one hand, he stubbornly refuses to go into the hospital until this work is complete, asking me over and over, 'What's next? What have we missed?' On the other, all his reserve has fallen away. From not speaking of it at all, he now mentions them taking his leg off at least five times a day – how much longer can he hold out? The gangrene must be growing and spreading like a filthy rot every day that he delays. I envy him his lack of smell; the place is putrid. I have to steel myself for the onslaught of the stink. This morning I had to step outside and gag. But this job has to be done. Intriguingly, he has referred to a task he hopes I will undertake for him.

This afternoon I uncovered a box of photographs and we spent a couple of hours sorting through them. Some had notes on the back; a date and sometimes a location. Hammond and Vivian in happier times on their honeymoon in Crete in 1934. There were a couple of his grandparents, Madame and Monsieur Rousseau, and images of Hammond as a small boy with his mother, Camille, and some of the factory staff, some thirty people, assembled in front of *Parfumerie Rousseau.*

'What else can you see?' he kept asking, only to be irritated by holiday snaps of Egypt. Finally I found at least one of the photographs he was looking for. It was of a woman with curly dark hair, attractive but not quite beautiful, with a sincere gaze to the camera. She was alone, so perhaps he had taken the photograph. As I described her, his face softened. 'That is Sylvie,' he said. 'Keep that one aside, I want you to take care of it. Also the one of my grandparents and that one of the staff and my mother. Take care of those ones. She should have those.'

'Who? Vivian?'

'Vivian?!' he barked. 'I'm telling you to hold onto them. Keep them *away* from Vivian. Don't let her so much as know of their *existence*. She'll be crawling through here like *vermin*.'

I reassured him they were safe with me. He calmed down but he was in too much pain to go on. He asked the time and cursed that it was only ten to the hour when Menna would come and give him the next morphine injection. Fortunately she came a little early and he was relieved of his burden of pain for another hour or so. Why on earth doesn't he just go into the hospital and get it over with? I can't imagine living with the unbearable pain and the knowledge that my flesh was slowly dying. It's too awful to contemplate but with this purging of the past it seems as though he is not confident that he will survive.

Dining at the villa has become a terrible strain for a variety of reasons. With the slippery sisters and Geraldson gone, it is now just Vivian, Jonathan, Mrs Somerville and myself. So, it's not just the ordeal of eating together and making conversation with nothing in common. Now I am often put upon to make up a four for bridge afterwards when I would much prefer to be tucked up in bed with my book – especially as I still have a hundred pages of *Madame Bovary* to finish.

Vivian yearns to see the back of me and never misses an opportunity to make thinly veiled comments to that effect. She seems to have forgotten that, unlike the other secretaries she

THE FRENCH PERFUMER

hired, I have successfully completed the task. This evening at dinner, Jonathan asked me what I was up to down in the cottage these days. Not because he is interested, but simply sensitive to any irritation suffered by Vivian. I explained that there were all sorts of bits and pieces to clear up, sounding rather lame and apologetic even to my own ears.

'Just pottering about, are we?' asked Vivian, her tone aggressively offhand.

'I expect we'll be finished very soon.'

'This week?' she asked. 'It really is too much of Hammond to expect —'

'Vivian, dear, don't upset yourself further,' Jonathan interrupted.

'I am not upsetting *myself*,' she snapped.

Mrs Somerville perked up her ears and looked at me sympathetically. 'Honey, why not come back to New York with me? I could do with an assistant to sort out my affairs.'

'Mrs Somerville,' said Jonathan in mock surprise. 'How many affairs are you engaged in? Do the gentlemen in question know there are others?'

Mrs Somerville squawked enthusiastically; she adores Jonathan's flirtatious teasing. I was unamused, seething in fact. I loathe the implication that I am some sort of servant to be passed from one spoiled wealthy person to another. Or some nuisance Vivian needs help to unload.

I should add that the highlight of the evening was the appearance of the Corsican walking past the dining-room windows, carrying two mink coats. A surprising development! Vivian rushed off to usher him into her office but the sight of the minks, *sans* the sisters, had a sobering effect on the remaining party.

While Vivian can do no wrong in Jonathan's eyes, I could see he was a little embarrassed as Mrs Somerville visibly put two and two together. 'Oh my, I hope the gals are all right,' she murmured. She hurriedly finished her meal, made her excuses and went to her room. I doubt she'll be tempted to leave without settling her bill.

Chapter Thirteen

I can hardly bring myself to write the words on this page. Hammond Brooke is dead. Even writing them does not make it real. I feel such pain. Such terrible heartache, but I must attempt to make sense of this dreadful night.

I had got to bed quite early and was almost asleep when there was a tap on the door. I opened it to find Menna there. She beckoned me to come with her, whispering, '*C'est Monsieur.*'

I slipped on my shoes and jacket and followed her down the back stairs and across the orchard, wondering what on earth could have happened. Once in the cottage, she ushered me into Mr Brooke's room which was strangely chapel-like, lit by candles and filled with great bunches of flowers from the garden.

Father Furolo, Monsieur Lapointe and the old doctor were all in the room. Mr Brooke lay so quietly in his bed I thought he had already gone but he beckoned me to come closer. The stench of his wounds was overwhelming but I didn't hesitate to accept his offered hand.

'Iris. My dear. I've never said this to you, but now is the time to say what we must say. You've made my last days much happier than they would have otherwise been. I was waiting for a messenger. One I could trust. You were sent to me.' He gave a wry smile. 'It has to some extent restored my faith in God and just in the nick of time.'

Thick grief rose in my throat. I was choking back tears and mumbling disjointed sentiments but he stopped me. 'I mentioned that I have one last task for you.' He felt around on his bedside table until he found an envelope that he pressed between his palms to check the contents. 'In here is a key and the address of my bank; there's a letter instructing them to allow you to access my safe deposit box. Everything you need is there. I beg you, don't discuss this with anyone. The only people you can trust are in this room. Apart from Sylvie. You can trust Sylvie; tell her everything that has happened. I have every faith in you, Iris Turner.' He leaned back on his pillows. 'There's nothing more to be done now.'

Father Furolo moved to the bedside and I stepped back to stand beside Menna, shocked to realise that he was administering the last rites. He said his goodbyes to Mr Brooke with obvious deep affection. Dr Renaud spoke quietly to Menna and then to Mr Brooke. He and Father Furolo left the room and moments later I heard the front door close.

'You don't have to stay, Iris,' said Mr Brooke. 'But I'd like to have you here. There's no risk of you being implicated.' Monsieur Lapointe knelt at his bedside and wept. Mr Brooke touched his friend's head and they spoke together in low voices for a long time.

Menna put on a pair of cotton gloves and spent a few moments preparing something from the medical kit I had previously seen in the kitchen. She returned to Mr Brooke's bedside with a hypodermic syringe and carefully placed it in his hand. He spoke to her with warm affection as she opened his shirt and laid his belly bare in readiness. She kissed his forehead and whispered her goodbyes.

Mr Brooke pushed the needle into his flesh and slowly depressed the syringe plunger. He lay back and sighed. He smiled and closed his eyes. His breathing, low and even, became shallow. Within an hour he had passed away and in the moment of his passing the wretched smell of the last weeks gave way to a tide of scents; joyous harmonies melded together in a fragrant symphony. The *parfumeur* was at peace.

Once he had gone, we went our separate ways. Each of us knew that the day ahead would be difficult as we fabricated our response to the news that our master had passed away in the night.

It was his choice, his timing, his need to control the situation and I respect that. There was nothing left for him in this world. But I feel so utterly bereft. He was a difficult, cranky old thing but for all his faults and frustrating ways, I came to love the man.

Today was more testing than any of us could have anticipated. I was woken by the sound of Vivian's screaming which swept through the house like a siren. I threw on some clothes and ran downstairs, passing Mrs Somerville, who stood outside her room in a robe and curlers. 'Oh my lord! What on earth's happening?'

I could hear Vivian shouting hoarsely, '*Le salaud!* The bastard! *Bastard!*' She began wailing and shouting in French. Jonathan was trying to calm her but it was having the opposite effect.

We arrived in the entry hall to the sight of him trying to physically restrain her. Monsieur Lapointe stood in the doorway. It must have been he who broke the news. His expression was one of distaste. The job done, he turned and walked away. Vivian caught sight of Menna leaving the kitchen and began shouting at her. Amandine hovered in the background until Madame Bouchard came out and pulled her back into the kitchen.

'Who helped him? Who? Who?! Someone helped him!' Vivian looked straight at me. 'It was *you!*' She broke Jonathan's hold and launched herself at me. Grabbing me by the shoulders she shook me hard. 'It was *you!* I know it was *you!*'

Mrs Somerville shouted at her to stop. I tried to break away but she had a tight hold on me and I was disoriented by the shaking. Jonathan gave up trying to reason with her and attempted to pull her away. 'Vivian, dear – calm down.'

Menna entered the fray, grasped Vivian's wrists and dragged her off me. In a blind rage, Vivian swung around and struck Menna hard across the face. 'Get out! Get out of this house! *Va-t-en! Sors d'ici – maintenant!*' Menna walked away, down the hall and toward the back of the house.

'Vivian, Vivian, please. It's all right.' Jonathan, looking thoroughly shaken, put his arms around her. The fight had gone out of her and he was able to half carry her into the office and shut the door. Mrs Somerville and I were left alone, too stunned to speak. We could hear Jonathan's soothing tones and the sound of Vivian's uncontrollable sobbing – shocking in itself. Before we could escape, Jonathan reappeared. 'You'll have to forgive her, she's in shock. It seems Mr Brooke died in his sleep last night. Please forget what she said. In fact, just forget this happened. Don't speak of it to anyone. Perhaps call the doctor – could you?'

He directed this request at me.

'To see Mr Brooke – or Vivian?' I asked.

'Well, both, but no rush to see Hammond, obviously. Ask him to bring something for Viv. Then he can sort the other business out.' He took a deep breath and went back into the office. There was something new in his bearing; a sense of purpose. A man whose time had come.

I called Dr Renaud from the hall phone. Fortunately his English is better than my French. I explained the situation, telling him the news he already knew.

I went down to Menna's room where she was neatly packing her few clothes into an old cardboard suitcase and trembling from head to foot. I had no idea what to do but I knew we both had to leave, immediately. Where could we go? What would Menna do now? I hardly knew where to start but began to quickly formulate a plan. I asked her to wait for me. She nodded and I left her there and hurried to my room. Having half packed my suitcase on several previous occasions due to Vivian's mercurial temperament, it wasn't difficult to quickly complete the job.

I left my suitcase in Menna's room and went off to find Monsieur Lapointe, who looked as miserable as I felt, and asked him to drive us to Nice. He set off to fetch the car while I rushed back upstairs and said my goodbyes to Mrs Somerville. We would find an inn or cheap hotel somewhere in Nice, I told her, just until I could work out what to do. She cut a tragic figure, sitting on her bed still in her robe, headscarf askew, curlers unravelling. She scrabbled through her handbag, all the time murmuring about how dreadful the situation was, and finally pulled out a thick roll of francs in a rubber band that she pressed into my hand.

'Thank you, Mrs Somerville, but I don't need this.' I handed it back. 'I have money.'

'Give it to the black girl, then – she'll need something to keep her going.' She was right and so I took the money and thanked her.

I was torn as to whether to tell Jonathan that we were leaving but, as it was, he was still in the office with Vivian and I didn't want to risk another kerfuffle. I dithered for a moment outside the door and could hear him speaking slowly and calmly to her. 'It could take years to settle it all.' Vivian's response was muffled but Jonathan continued. 'Viv, you need to be careful what you say. Don't start something that could get out of hand.' I slipped away then; I had nothing to say to either of them.

Monsieur Lapointe had brought the car around and put our suitcases in the front seat. Menna looked so frightened, I wondered how long it had been since she left the property. I opened the door for her to get in. She glanced around anxiously as though some alternative might present itself but it didn't and, with heavy reluctance, she got in the car.

Although I was preparing myself to leave in the not-too-distant future, the circumstances and the speed of the exit were shocking. As we left the villa behind, it tore at my heart that Mr Brooke still lay in his bed, neglected but not forgotten. Now he has gone, my loyalty to him burns brighter than ever. Whatever his final wishes are, I will dedicate myself to completing them in his honour.

To find a hotel that would accept Menna as a guest was much more difficult than I imagined. It was obviously no surprise to Monsieur Lapointe, who waited patiently outside each establishment. In the end, I asked to use a hotel telephone and called

Alexander. He urged us to come immediately – he had more than enough room and would be delighted to host us. I gave Monsieur Lapointe the address and he drove us to the village of Mougins in the hills above Cannes. My French was not up to the task of explaining to Menna where we were going. She sat quietly with no apparent expectations. It seemed that she too has faith in me.

We arrived at Alexander's somewhat disoriented but he is an overwhelmingly kind host and his house comfortable and spacious without being ostentatious. I gave him the barest explanation of the events leading up to our departure and he was very solicitous of us both, making sure that Menna also felt welcome. He had his rather stern Scottish housekeeper, Mrs K, show us to our rooms. She didn't blink an eye at having a coloured guest but I expect she would need to be fairly liberal-minded to run this household. After a long bath and a brief nap before dinner, I feel better equipped to discuss the situation and make some plans. It will be a relief to dine with a friend this evening.

Menna insisted on eating in the kitchen this evening which is understandable. It all became terribly awkward and I am just not sure what is right. She had such a bond with Mr Brooke, not to mention losing her home and job on top of everything else. I have no idea how long she worked there; possibly years. Nor do I know what will become of her now – or even if I can help.

Alexander sat down at the kitchen table and patiently asked her questions, hoping to find out where her family were or even if she had family in France. She kept her gaze trained on a point over his shoulder, only once glancing across at me. I gave her a reassuring smile but her eyes slid away and she maintained her silence. You have to hand it to her for self-discipline.

Freddy had been expected for supper but in the circumstances Alexander kindly telephoned and put him off until tomorrow evening. It was nice to share a quiet meal and discuss what had happened with Vivian. Naturally I did not mention being present at Mr Brooke's passing.

'Well, your solicitor fellow's comment about it being an odd situation has come to pass in more ways than one,' Alexander said. 'If there were more sex and less death, it would qualify as a French farce.' I asked what he thought about Menna's situation and if we could help her find work. 'Algerian, you said. *Sans papiers,* no doubt. There are tens of thousands of undocumented Africans in France, especially since the war. Without knowing where her family is . . .'

'I feel partly responsible for what happened.'

'I don't see why. It sounds as though Vivian was determined to be rid of you both. It was only Brooke holding you there.'

I assured him that we would be leaving as soon as possible but he insisted we should stay as long as we wished. He would ask around discreetly about work for Menna. He suggested I place a call to Mr Hubert and have him organise my passage home, which seemed sensible since it was part of the agreement. I made some excuses to get down to Cannes tomorrow from where I will take the train to Monaco to deal with this business for Mr Brooke. Then I would be free to go home.

These next couple of days will almost certainly be my last in France and I wanted to see William one last time. I found his name easily in the phone book and telephoned him at home. He sounded subdued but agreed to meet me tomorrow morning in

Nice. I was trembling as I hung up the phone. I only wish I knew what had happened between us and why it is so difficult. Even if tomorrow is the last time I will ever gaze on his dear face, I am so looking forward to it. Just to be with him for a few minutes.

As I was preparing for bed just now, I realised I still had the money Mrs Somerville had given me. I knocked on Menna's door. She opened it nervously and I could see she hadn't touched a thing in her room or even sat on the bed by the looks of it. I stumbled through an explanation and placed the thick roll of notes in her hand. She stared at it with alarm and pushed it back to me but I insisted. She slipped it in her pocket and whispered, '*Merci, ma sœur.*'

If only we could communicate. I sense such grief and sadness in her, I am almost certain she has been scarred by some tragedy. She is so alone in the world. We are both so alone in the world, but the difference between our situations is immense.

Menna has gone. She slipped away in the night. I was on my way to breakfast just now when I noticed her door ajar, her bed undisturbed, her suitcase gone. I came back to my room and sat on my bed and cried. I expect she had her reasons and I couldn't hope to understand them. I am certain I shall never see her again.

Mrs K kindly drove me down to the station in Cannes this morning and when my train pulled into Nice, William stood waiting on the platform, heartbreakingly handsome in a double-breasted suit and trilby. He kissed my cheek and guided me out into the street and into a small café near the station. We sat down and ordered coffee. It was just us, face-to-face, no distractions, but all I could pick up was a prickling discomfort between us. The air was thick with the unsaid, perhaps the unsayable. I explained that Mr Brooke had died and without going into too much detail, told the story of Vivian's final explosion at which he was highly indignant on my behalf.

'It will certainly be interesting to find out the terms of the will,' he said. 'It's fortunate they have no children. Vivian could have found herself evicted by her nearest and dearest.'

'She would have tamed them into submission long before now,' I said, and we shared a smile. Something hung in the air between us, something we couldn't address. Although we chatted amiably, I couldn't help but be saddened that this was our last time together and yet we couldn't crack the surface tension. I was struck by the thought that I will never meet a man as good as William again. I sense in him almost untold depths of kindness and I so longed to love him. He had to get back to his office and I said briskly that I too must be off.

He walked me back to Gare de Nice in silence and took the trouble to come onto the platform to wait for the train. There were ten painfully awkward minutes of diminishing small talk but still he stayed and I didn't want him to leave. As my train approached, he ducked in for a goodbye peck but our lips met in a passionate kiss and we were clinging to one another for dear life and I didn't even care if I missed this train or the next – or spent the rest of my life on that platform held tight in his arms. He pulled away abruptly and hurried off down the platform without another word or parting glance.

Now here I am on the train going toward Monaco, blind to the blue beauty of the Mediterranean as it slides past. I feel nothing but pain as the miles separate us and the thread that binds us unspools. I have left something so precious behind.

Leaving everything and everyone has been frenetic. I haven't had a moment for my journal until now, alone on the train to Paris with plenty of time to record the extraordinary happenings of the last few days.

After leaving William last Thursday, I arrived in Monte Carlo feeling confused and upset. Whenever we met, he appeared every bit as besotted as myself. I had made the assumption that Topsy's boredom was the catalyst for their liaison – a theory for which I had no proof. I wondered if perhaps she had a stronger hold on his heart than I thought? I cursed myself for not being one of these wily types with the ability to lure men away from other women – I would do it! William is a man worth fighting for.

I had no interest in being in Monte Carlo other than my mission. In different circumstances, I would have liked to wander the streets brushing shoulders with the wealthy and celebrated, hoping to catch a glimpse of Princess Grace. But as it was, I took myself directly to the bank.

It wasn't the type of high-street bank with which I was familiar; more grand and hushed, with a doorman. Beyond a marble foyer was a large room with a reception desk attended by a woman in a smart business suit. I approached her and presented my letter of authority. She left her desk and consulted a man in an adjacent office. The man read the letter and came straight out.

He introduced himself as Monsieur Dufour and (in impeccable English) invited me into his office. He asked if I had any form of identification, apologising for the necessary formality. Fortunately I had my passport with me in preparation for my departure, which he glanced over and handed back. The woman returned and placed a manila folder on his desk. He read some notes in the folder and finally said, 'I understand that you will take the entire contents of the safe deposit box and it will subsequently no longer be required.'

I wasn't sure about that but explained that Monsieur Brooke had passed away and I was now carrying out his wishes.

'I'm very sorry to hear that news. The Rousseau family have been valued clients of the bank for many years,' he said.

He escorted me to a stately room with a heavy vault door. He withdrew the box itself and placed it on the desk, explaining that the door would be locked and, until such time as I pressed the button, I would have complete privacy.

When he had gone, I opened the box to find four items inside. The first was a thick cream envelope with the words *Testament de Hammond Auguste Brooke* typed on it. The second was a book-shaped parcel wrapped in brown paper. The third was a small package addressed to me; the fourth an envelope also addressed to me, which I opened. Inside was a wad of francs and a letter in his spidery script:

My dear Iris,

You have no doubt realised by now that you are in possession of something precious, beyond monetary value. I know you understand the vital importance of these two items which is why I have entrusted you alone to carry out my last wishes.

Do not let anyone know these items are in your possession.

Please deliver my will and the ledger to Sylvie Moreau,

Université Paris Descartes, Rue de l'École-de-Médecine, Quartier de l'Odéon, Paris.

I have enclosed some cash to cover expenses and have also left you a small gift, the proceeds of which may be helpful to you.

Once you have completed that task, you are free of all obligation but I hope you will think of me fondly from time to time.

All my best, yours Hammond

The writing swerved and swooped across several pages. It was heartbreaking to realise that these last weeks Mr Brooke had been quietly preparing for his death. But most of all, I felt honoured to be chosen for the task.

I opened the large package. While I was not in a laughing mood, I couldn't help myself. I joined Hammond Brooke in having the last laugh. It was a bulky leather-bound ledger, the cover scuffed and worn from the hands of three generations of Rousseau perfumers. Its pages released an exquisite combination of scents, as though working in fragrant accord.

The old devil. I wondered what else he had in store but decided to wait to open my gift in my own time. I rewrapped the ledger, tucked the other items in my handbag and pressed the button.

Monsieur Dufour came and released me. 'Just out of curiosity,' I asked him, 'can you tell me when this was deposited?' He looked a little affronted, so perhaps one is not supposed to ask that question. Nevertheless, he asked me to wait a moment and went back to his office. He returned a few minutes later. 'Monsieur Brooke secured that particular box in April 1949 and the only access since that date was two weeks ago.' I thanked him and went on my way.

Monte Carlo is constructed like an amphitheatre facing the harbour, and that day a cool breeze whipped through the twisting streets, threatening rain. On the way back to the station, I bought a small attaché case to keep my precious cargo safe and dry.

I wanted to set off to Paris immediately. Mr Brooke had provided more than enough funds to cover my travel and accommodation so I would not bother Mr Hubert. I had thought I would attend the funeral, which must be any day, but now I had the holy grail in my possession that seemed unwise. When I arrived back in Cannes I bought a ticket for Paris to leave the next morning.

As soon as I got back to Alexander's I went straight to my room and opened the gift from Mr Brooke. Inside the first wrapping was a box and inside that was an item carefully wrapped in one of his fine linen monogrammed handkerchiefs. It was a 100-gram flask of his rose absolute. I knew from my audit that this was an extraordinarily generous gift – worth hundreds of pounds. Tucked into the box was a *Document de Certification*.

I found Alexander and let him know that I would depart the next day. He immediately conceived a plan for a farewell dinner and before I could protest, rushed off to make the arrangements. I had a long bath but hardly felt equal to the task of entertaining guests – let alone as the centre of attention. Fortunately Freddy arrived in high spirits with his violin (quite recovered from its soaking) so I was off that particular hook. Topsy and Sebastian turned up. William sent apologies.

Alexander went all out to create a night to remember. The weather had held and the dining table outside was splendidly set by Mrs K and we sipped champagne looking out over the garden and pool. I already felt nostalgia for the gauzy dusk of Riviera summers that would never be mine again. As night fell the most beautiful illuminations lit up the tall palms around the perimeter of the property. It was touching to see how proud Alexander was of his house. He is so often dismissive of these things but I expect that's because of the associated sting of his exile in paradise.

Mrs K seemed to be held in high esteem by all present and had no problem delivering an extravagant spread at short notice. Over the meal there was a great deal of speculation about Mr Brooke that I didn't participate in, not quite trusting myself. According to Sebastian, his death had been kept quiet. The expat community had heard about it through the grapevine but it had somehow been kept from the press. The funeral was to be a private service.

As Mrs K served the dessert, which I recall was rice pudding, she murmured discreetly that there was someone to see me. I excused myself and hurried inside, thinking perhaps Menna had returned. Who should I find waiting at the front door but William!

He was clearly nervous and ill at ease, very unlike his normal self. Apologising, he beckoned me to come outside and led me down the path beside the house into the shadows of the back garden. He stopped and took my hands in his. Then, just as quickly, he dropped them as if not appropriate.

'I wanted to tell you the truth today but my courage failed me,' he began. 'I don't know what you'll think of me.'

'Nothing could change my opinion of you, William.'

'I doubt that.' He plunged his hands gloomily into his pockets. The suspense was unbearable.

'Is it related to Topsy, by any chance?' I asked.

'You knew? Of course. Nothing escapes you.'

'I sensed something, that's all.'

'The truth is, while I was sent out here by my firm, through a complicated series of blunders – not of my creation – I was dismissed. Rather than return to London under a cloud and find another job, Topsy suggested I go out on my own, as a sort of financial consultant. She introduced me to one of her wealthy friends and I did some cost analysis work. Nothing ground-breaking, but the fellow seemed happy enough. He referred me to a chum of his and, quite quickly, there was pressure on me to appear as successful as my potential clients. Topsy insisted I needed better clothes and a snazzy car that she financed to get things rolling.' He paused, although this clearly wasn't the end of the story. 'She was bored and lonely – I was a diversion. A pro-ject, I suppose. I've never been in love with her but I wouldn't hurt her for the world. I'm grateful to her. I feel beholden.'

'She doesn't own you, though. You could still come back to England and start again.'

William gave a dry laugh. 'If I walk away now it's with the clothes on my back. My earnings have never kept pace. But that's not it. My real concern is that she's very emotional. She knows how I feel about you.'

I was flattered by this admission. 'You told her?'

'I talked to her, you know, after that evening we spent in Valbonne. She was much more upset than I imagined. She insis-ted she would leave Sebastian, bring it all out in the open —'

'She doesn't want to lose you.'

He turned away angrily. 'Perhaps, but somehow I don't think so. She doesn't like having things taken from her. Sebastian is my cousin. Our mothers are sisters. The fallout would be catas-trophic for everyone. Besides, I don't want to marry her. I should never have got involved in the first place. I'm entirely to blame. I despise myself. I'm shackled through my own foolishness.'

'And that's what you came here to tell me?'

'I didn't want you to go back to England thinking it was something else, something you did or said. Some imperfection. Nothing could be further from the truth, Iris. I wanted you to know.'

Despite the warm evening, I felt chilled. I wanted to go inside and take my suitcase and leave. Not even say goodbye to any of them. I realised Alexander and Freddy probably knew the situation and thought me silly and naïve. But that wasn't so important. I felt nothing but compassion for William, who had been blinded, as one can so easily be, by the wealth and glamour that was all around us. Neither he nor I belong in that world. We were meant for some simpler, more wholesome, life – but that is clearly not to be.

When I first saw him waiting there at the door, I secretly hoped he had come to declare himself. As though I imagined myself as the heroine in the final scene of a romantic film. How foolish and presumptuous of me. I thanked him and told him that I appreciated his honesty. He wished me a good voyage. We said goodbye like strangers. I won't write or speak of William ever again but I will never forget a single moment of our time together.

I was able to slip back to my place almost unnoticed under the cover of a riotous conversation relating to the slippery sisters. I had told Alexander the story the previous day and he was regaling the group with an exaggerated version of this tale.

Freddy was familiar with the duo. 'Ladies of the night in every sense of the expression, so I understand. Although business must be slow these days; only the most undiscerning gentleman wants to get naughty with a nag.'

'I thought Madame Brooke only accepted Debrett-sanctioned guests,' said Topsy, only half joking. She gave me a stiff smile and I was almost certain she knew William had been there. It really didn't matter any more. I felt some sympathy for her. I have come to realise that Sebastian is one of those men who are full of boyish enthusiasms and his pampered life reads like an extended list to Santa. He is frivolous and insubstantial. Everything William is not.

Discussion about the sisters fired Freddy's imagination. He leapt to his feet, seized his violin and launched into an amusing rendition of Elvis Presley's 'One Night with You' concerning the sisters' nocturnal activities. It became increasingly vulgar and I hoped Mrs K couldn't hear from the kitchen. I crept away and went to bed.

I had a wretched night and woke early. The house was silent; all signs of the dinner party – including the guests – had vanished. Mrs K was still at the helm and made me porridge topped with a crust of brown sugar and a lick of butter. It tasted like home and I almost wept with homesickness. Alexander and the gang had all gone out late last night, she told me, and not returned as yet, which was really too bad.

She drove me down to the train, my new attaché case gripped tightly on my lap. I wasn't in the mood for conversation but, out of courtesy, asked her how she came to be there. She explained that she had been the housekeeper at Alexander's family's estate in the Scottish border county of Berwickshire for many years. 'The family lived in London but they would come up two or three times a year. Christmas always. I got to know Alexander very well over the years. He's a lovely lad. In my line of work, you need to curb your curiosity. There's nothing worse than a nosy housekeeper but when people argue and shout, you can't help but overhear things you shouldn't. So I knew he had been sent away. Not long after he arrived here, he wrote me a fair tragic letter, begged me to come and take care of him. So here I am.'

'He's lucky to have you.'

'Of course he is,' she said. 'He has many admirable traits but common sense is not among them.'

As I got out of the car at the station she said, 'He'll be sad to have missed saying goodbye. He's very fond of you.'

And so I departed, without goodbyes, leaving behind some who meant nothing to me and one or two for whom I held a real fondness. And one I loved with all my heart. None of whom I will ever see again. To be honest, the one I was quite delighted to leave behind was *Madame Bovary*.

Chapter Fourteen

I had no hotel booking in Paris but took a taxi from Gare de Lyon to the Rue de l'École-de-Médecine. It was late afternoon and my plan was to check into a hotel near to the university so I could locate Sylvie Moreau the next morning and, with any luck, take an afternoon train to Calais. The taxi driver helpfully located a little hotel not far from the university and I took a room there.

I freshened up and sat on the bed and thought about everything that had happened. It was actually too much to take in. I desperately wanted to complete this final task and go home to the familiarity of England. I yearned for the musty old smells of home that I had been so dismissive of a few months earlier. Rather than wasting away the time in my room, it seemed advisable to at least make some enquiries. Taking the attaché case with me, I walked down to the Université Paris Descartes.

The exterior of the university gave no hint of the grandeur of the interior with its wide hallways and vaulted stone ceilings and I felt increasingly intimidated by the task of finding Sylvie

Moreau in this imposing building. I stopped several people and made enquiries without success.

Finally an older man directed me to an administrative office where a woman was in the process of locking up for the night. After several attempts she grasped what I was saying and explained something in such rapid-fire French I couldn't understand a single word. With obvious irritation she tried more slowly and this time I understood that Sylvie had *gone*. She no longer worked there. Until that moment I thought this transaction would be relatively simple. Suddenly it was impossible and (to both our surprise) I burst into tears.

Alarmed by this turn of events, the woman patted my arm and made soothing sounds. Unlocking the door, she beckoned me inside, sat me down and poured me a small brandy. She chatted on, presumably reassuring me that all was recoverable, while she rattled through various filing drawers. Finally locating the correct file, she flipped through until she found a folder and, muttering under her breath, examined the contents. She picked up the phone and dialled. We waited. Then she began to speak. Given we only met five minutes ago she found an awful lot to say to the person on the other end. She handed me the phone and, like a miracle, a voice said, 'Yes? I am Sylvie.'

We spoke only for a few minutes; as soon as I mentioned Mr Brooke she said I should come straight away. I passed the phone back to the woman, who took down the address for me. She was now pleased with herself and solicitous. Providing me with a small map, she walked me out to the street and set me off in the right direction.

I recognised Sylvie as soon as she opened the door – and was immediately annoyed with myself as I had left the photographs

Mr Brooke wanted me to give her back at the hotel. She was older than the photo, perhaps mid- to late-forties but had an energy about her, an animation that would not be captured on film.

She warmly invited me in, immediately asking after Mr Brooke and so I had to break the news without delay that he had passed away. She sat down abruptly at the kitchen table and wept inconsolably. A young girl of perhaps twelve came running from another room and stopped and stared at me furiously. She wrapped herself around her mother, murmuring questions. Sylvie held her close and spoke softly to her. The girl paled but didn't cry, only held her mother more tightly. I wished I could leave them in peace.

After a few minutes Sylvie stood up, excused herself and left the room. The girl sat and stared at me. When Sylvie returned she had regained her composure. She offered me coffee or wine. I elected wine although the brandy was still sweet in my mouth. We sat at the table and, as instructed, I explained the full circumstances of Hammond Brooke's death. Sylvie listened with stoicism, asking the occasional question and urging me to continue when I faltered toward the end of the story.

When I had finished and answered all her questions, I lifted the ledger out of the attaché case and placed it on the table. Sylvie gave a heartfelt sigh, her hands clasped at her lips. 'We never touch this book. This is sacred.'

The girl pulled it toward her, opening it with a sense of casual propriety. Sylvie was explaining something about the ledger but my attention was drawn to the girl as she turned the pages, glancing at the compositions with interest. When she reached the last page she turned the book toward me, pointing to the name of the final fragrance. '*Je suis Aurélie.*'

And I found myself staring into Hammond Brooke's storm-grey eyes. Yes. Of course. This was Aurélie. His last and only hope.

By the time I left Sylvie's apartment it was after 10 p.m. The prospect of my tiny hotel room was not very inviting and this was my last night in Paris – who knows if I will ever return. I stopped at a small café and ordered a glass of rosé. Now as I sit here to complete my final entry in this journal, I'm still stunned by Aurélie's existence, with only a vague sense of the implications. I want to try and connect the strands of the story to make sense of it all.

I gave Sylvie the will, half expecting her to open it immediately – perhaps because I was curious! She put it aside and instead asked if I would stay and share a meal with them. I agreed and we sat down together over salad and cold meats.

Sylvie was interested to know the circumstances of my involvement. Aurélie listened attentively as I explained the situation and, although she didn't attempt to speak in English, she obviously understood much of what I was saying. After the meal, she took the ledger to the adjoining living room and sat down on the floor to read it while Sylvie told me at least some of her story.

Sylvie had trained as a chemist and joined the laboratory staff of *Parfumerie Rousseau* in 1936. As she explained it, she didn't work with Hammond Brooke or even have contact with him as he was elevated to a degree where he didn't deal with the day-to-day business, simply the creations. The only time she had contact with him was when she and the two other chemists presented drafts for his approval. These meetings, she said with a smile, were often fraught because of his high standards and short temper.

His grandfather, Monsieur Rousseau, was still alive at that time and Sylvie described him as a kind man but also demanding and uncompromising. He cared deeply for his staff but treated Hammond like a prince, which made his grandson less than popular with staff. Nevertheless they could not help but be awed by the younger man's genius as a composer and his ability to identify hundreds, if not thousands, of different elements. He was able to smell a draft and identify a single note that should be added or eliminated which would transform the fragrance.

'He was born for this job,' she said. Knowing a little of Mr Brooke's story, I wondered if she meant 'bred', although both are true, but she tapped her nose and pointed to her daughter in the other room. 'She has the same.'

When I asked about Vivian's involvement in the business, Sylvie's expression clouded. 'When I arrive, yes, she is involved. She is very beautiful. *Sophistiquée*. But she is a tyrant. If people don't do what she wants, she is very angry.'

It seems that after she married Hammond in 1934, Vivian worked in the sales part of the company. In that capacity, she was often away in various parts of the world, particularly Saudi Arabia, where through her aristocratic connections she was able to insinuate herself with the Saudi royal family and, by association, other wealthy families. But the novelty of the work quickly wore off for Vivian and by the time Sylvie joined the firm a year later, it was rumoured that Madame Brooke did more socialising and spending than actual selling and there was growing tension between the elderly Monsieur Rousseau and his granddaughter-in-law. Given that the family all lived together at Villa Rousseau, one could imagine these tensions must have spilled over to home.

Sometime in the year prior to the war breaking out, Vivian took herself off for an extended trip home to England and then to Germany. She returned somewhat enamoured of the Führer, with whom she had become personally acquainted, and deeply impressed by the economic affluence he had brought to Germany.

'Before this, people at the factory were *discrets*. We respect the private world of the family,' explained Sylvie. 'But at this time, when Madame Brooke came back from Germany, this changed. There were Jewish people working there who knew the truth of what was happening. There was a Polish cook at the villa; she was very afraid. She told the chauffeur, Monsieur Lapointe, of the conversations in the house. He is also the driver for the business and he hears many conversations in the car. So everyone knows Madame Brooke has sympathy with this terrible Hitler.'

I asked Sylvie if she knew what Mr Brooke thought of all this at the time.

'I think he listens to Vivian's opinions but he doesn't care about politics. He doesn't care about anything he cannot smell. He held a fascination for anything that did smell. He had his head up in the cloud – always. He is the artist. Vivian liked to dance and to visit the casino but at that time he will never go where there is smoking. This is very bad for the nose – smoking is never allowed at the villa. People say she has a *liaison* with other men. So this is not good for the family who have great respect from everyone.

'So, the workers were very happy when Madame Brooke went away. We know this is not her decision but that of Madame and Monsieur Rousseau. They are people of great honour. They have a *dévotion* for France and belief in *liberté, égalité, fraternité*. They have no sympathy for these *fascistes*.'

The Rousseau household began hosting Jewish friends and colleagues fleeing Paris. 'Many Jews were coming from the north, not just escaping the Occupied Zone but Vichy France as well. We hear stories that Jews are being sent away and murdered – this seemed impossible!

'Monsieur Rousseau came to me one day and said he had seen my fine handwriting. I thought – hmm, unusual, a compliment for me? He asked me some questions, about what I thought of the Jews. I said that I thought nothing, we are all French. He asked if I would help save the lives of some people. I said of course. This is how it started.'

It seems that Monsieur Rousseau realised that the resources the firm used for labelling and packaging perfume could be employed to create false documents for Jewish refugees; new identities that would allow them to cross the border into Italy or Spain.

'So then we would stay in the evening and make these together, the two of us. It was nice. We talk while we work. This work is delicate. It takes time but not as difficult as you might think because in France every *département* has some different documents. So we can make *certificats de naissance, carnet de rationnement, diplômes scolaires* to look very much *authentique*. At that time, I had no knowledge of what happens after this. Monsieur Rousseau does everything else. But then the Gestapo, they came to Villa Rousseau and everything changed.'

It was early 1943 when they arrived and searched the villa and grounds. Fortunately they found nothing incriminating but they liked what they saw and evicted the Rousseau family. Madame and Monsieur were forced to go and live with relatives in the nearby town of Menton. Madame Rousseau had suffered heart troubles for some years and within weeks of their eviction she passed away. Monsieur Rousseau, now almost eighty years old, also became unwell and was not able to continue the work with Sylvie.

'So this is the end of Hammond's golden life,' said Sylvie. 'He starts to live in a small apartment over the factory. Now there is no Free Zone, *les Boches* are our masters. So there are many, many Jews needing help for escape. Monsieur Rousseau wanted Hammond to take over this work. This is now more important than making perfume.'

Although Hammond respected his grandfather's wishes, he was apparently far from happy about it. He thought the Jews could look after themselves. His only interest was to keep the business going.

Then, a strange twist in the story occurred: Vivian reappeared in residence at Villa Rousseau, managing the house and entertaining the Gestapo top brass who used the villa as a retreat. Hammond was invited for a meal at his own home.

Sylvie said that he had attended out of curiosity. It was a surprise to be introduced as Vivian's brother but he played along. The last thing he wanted to do was raise any suspicions and so he aligned himself with Vivian, appearing sympathetic to the Nazi cause. The Gestapo must have been satisfied because orders for perfume began to arrive for wives back home in Germany. The business was now under the dubious protection of Vivian, but something had changed for Hammond Brooke.

'He was shocked by the things he heard that night. He realises the truth about these invaders; he woke up from his dream world. Now he understood the wish of his grandfather. So, then Hammond and myself, we work together in the night to make the papers.

'The driver, Didier Lapointe, he moves the people from one place to another. The building of the factory is a very old *château*. This building has tunnels into the town. Many places to hide people. We had many children hidden. Of course, by now there was *la filière* and *la résistance* – this part was growing. Some Jewish people could speak French but many cannot and children alone cannot cross a border. They are hungry and sick and the doctor of the Rousseau family came every day to treat them. The Italian *curé*, Monsieur Furolo, he takes the children by foot for hundreds of miles across *Italie* to *Yougoslavie*. In this he is helped by the people from many different *monastères*. People risk their lives.

'I came to know Hammond very well in this time. We spent many hours together working and we had some arguments and felt some fear but we also laugh and I came to love him. So then I was staying also in the little apartment. It was not safe to leave the factory late at night – there was a curfew.'

She explained that when the Gestapo came to the factory it was in force. They found nothing but must have had credible information because they set dynamite and destroyed most of the building. Hammond and Sylvie escaped and fled to Menton, where Monsieur Rousseau was still living.

'At that time, we rent an apartment near to Monsieur Rousseau and this is a very happy time for us. Here we discover we will have a baby and this made Hammond very happy. Monsieur Rousseau is also happy. Hammond is married to Vivian and in peacetime this is *le scandale* but in wartime – and no other child born in this family – this is different.'

Aurélie was born in January 1944 but less than a month later her parents had a late-night visitor. Didier came with information that Vivian had denounced Sylvie. He was certain that she knew nothing of their work but Sylvie posed a threat to Vivian's future – now she was using her influence to eliminate the problem. By the time the Gestapo arrived the next morning, Sylvie and Aurélie had been spirited across the border into Spain.

It was during this next year that Monsieur Rousseau and Hammond together created *Aurélie*. This collaboration, explained Sylvie, was an extraordinary event akin to a collaboration between Monet and Matisse or Strauss and Mozart. These men were recognised as the masters in their field.

While the approaches of the two perfumers may have differed, they were united by their objective: both equally determined to evoke something beautiful and pure amidst the tragic ruin of France. They shared a vision of a reborn France, as symbolised in the inherent promise of a child. A child born in the midst of despair and conflict: Aurélie.

Raw materials were difficult to procure. There were many visits to the ruins of the factory to scavenge for anything that survived. They did not have the luxury of plentiful materials to create dozens of drafts but had to draw on memory and imagine the combined effect. Their burning desire was to extract hidden potential from the depths, to illuminate and glorify the obscure.

By the time France was liberated, they had created a fragrance they believed worthy of what both men realised would be their final composition. Hammond's sight was now failing and in early 1945 Monsieur Rousseau passed away. The fragrance bible of *Parfumerie Rousseau* had originally travelled to Menton with Monsieur Rousseau and it would seem that once that final composition was recorded it was lodged, together with Hammond's will, in the safe deposit box in Monte Carlo.

The war was finally over. Sylvie and Aurélie, now fifteen months old, returned to France, initially to Paris where Sylvie was reunited with her own mother. In his letters Hammond had been adamant that by the time Sylvie returned, he would be divorced and they would marry. But with Hammond's loss of sight, things had become increasingly complicated. Vivian refused to grant a divorce and was still in possession of the villa. Although the family had been wealthy, their funds in French banks had been stolen. The villa itself had been quietly plundered – Vivian had been powerless to prevent the loss of many paintings and antiques. Hammond needed to start production of the new perfume to generate much-needed funds.

Shortly before Sylvie was to return to Grasse with Aurélie, she had a telegram from Hammond asking her to meet him at a hotel in Lyon instead. 'We stayed for three days in the hotel; it should have been the beginning of our life together but it was the end. Hammond told me that Vivian knew about our daughter and she was very angry. He said to me that she is dangerous, she has powerful friends. He doesn't want us to come to Grasse. He fears for Aurélie's life. He told me to go back to Paris and wait.

'I came to work at the *université* and gave that address. I don't want Vivian to find where I live. The letters from him become less because he cannot see but every month some money came to my bank to help us. The years pass, and he is too ill to travel, but what can we do?'

'Do you know what happened to the perfume – *Aurélie?*' I asked.

'I know this not from Hammond, but from my friend Hervé, who works at that time in the factory. It was, of course, very successful after the war when people needed something beautiful and magical in their life. But this was made exclusively by *Parfumerie Rousseau* in a little factory in Grasse. They could not make enough. The materials were very expensive but Hammond did not want to make this perfume for rich women and this was also the wish of his grandfather. *Aurélie* was to bring joy to ordinary women. Women who suffered in the war. Women who helped win the war.

'But, of course, Vivian's idea is not this. She needs money and wanted to sell the product to a big manufacturer. Hammond refused. She makes some threats to staff but only Hammond has the complete formulation. She makes a war with him about this. So, in the end, he said enough. And he stopped.'

Sylvie toyed with the envelope containing the will. 'Hammond has already told me about this document. Everything is for Aurélie. She will carry on the work. That is why Hammond asked you to bring it to me.'

'But what if she would prefer to do something else?'

She shook her head with a smile. 'When we meet in Lyon, Aurélie was one-and-a-half years old and we see already she had the gift. Everywhere she goes, she smells. Even when she is a baby she brings everything to the nose. She understands this world through smell. This makes Hammond very happy.'

But, even assuming that the villa now belonged to Aurélie, how would they evict Vivian when Hammond had failed? Would she have the resources to take legal action? She responded to this question with a shrug. 'This is what I hear: ever since the war these two have been at war. Vivian occupies the villa and

Hammond the little house. She makes money from the guests to continue there. Hammond was not able to make her leave – this is very complicated – but I think something will happen . . .'

About to tell me something more, Sylvie hesitated and glanced into the sitting room where Aurélie lay curled up on the floor asleep, one hand resting on the ledger. Excusing herself, Sylvie left me alone at the table and ushered her daughter off to bed. It was a gift to have a few moments to gather myself after the avalanche of information. Little did I know there were even more startling revelations ahead.

Sylvie returned and made us coffee. It was getting late but I felt in no hurry to leave. The kitchen opened onto a small balcony. We moved outside and sat in the velvety warmth of the summer night.

'Madame Brooke,' said Sylvie quietly, 'is not a French national. She is a war criminal – a collaborator. Do you know how she makes money during the war? No? She brings women in for the Gestapo. She makes this beautiful house of Rousseau *la maison de prostitution*.'

While this was obviously scandalous, it was not altogether surprising to me, given Vivian's mercenary nature. Why then, I asked Sylvie, had Vivian not been denounced?

'After the war people are angry,' said Sylvie. 'Women who were together with our enemy, they were punished with *humiliation*. The hair was cut off the head. Not Vivian. She has some *influence* with important people. Now I think it is too late for this. France has other things to think about. Something will happen, I don't know what. We must wait.'

We were both tired by then. It was time for me to leave. I told her I would post Hammond's photographs from England.

We parted affectionately and promised to keep in touch. But as I turned away from her door, one last question came to mind. 'Did you know the servant at the house, an Algerian woman named Menna?'

Despite sharing confidences all evening, Sylvie now looked guarded. 'I have heard about her,' she said quietly.

'Do you know where she came from, or if she had family?'

'I only know what people say. That Madame Brooke took her from the place of children with no mother or father . . .'

'Orphanage?'

'Yes, from an orphanage during the war. The girl was, I think, fourteen years old.'

'Vivian adopted her?'

'No. She gave money for her. To work in the villa. No one will work there. She wants that girl because she is silent. A person who cannot speak against her.'

'She owned her?'

'In France, we cannot own people – it's not possible. But maybe the girl does not know this.'

All I can hope is that Menna knows it now – that she has family somewhere and can somehow find them. I pray that she hasn't returned to the villa like a homing pigeon but flown far away from that place.

Walking back through the streets of Paris, my mind was alive with all these pieces of puzzle shifting into place. I knew there was no chance of sleep and needed to write every detail of this evening in my journal before it blurred and the detail was lost. Now the story is finished, I will return to my hotel and, in a few hours, watch the first light of dawn over the rooftops of Paris. Soon I will be on the train to Calais and finally home to Linnet

Lane, where I will put my key in the door and return to my former life. While I have changed irrevocably, my great fear is that everything will resume almost exactly as I left it. I must do everything in my power to resist; to live a wider, deeper existence.

Chapter Fifteen

Linnet Lane
September 1956

I had put this journal aside when I arrived home, in no mood to relive the experience of the last months. Today I sat down and read it from start to finish and reflected on the old Iris who arrived in the South of France those few short months ago.

The scope of my worldly experience was so limited, so restrained. I'm dazzled by my own daring. Fancy giving up a secure position for such an unlikely enterprise! I wonder if I was in my right mind, but I do remember the sense of desperation I felt back then, my loneliness and isolation. I didn't fully realise it at the time, but when Father died, my sense of purpose died with him. Caring for him was the centre of my existence and without that each day I was simply going through the motions. Colleen was right. I was barely living at all. My life was a narrow path trudging toward the final destination.

When I first returned home in July, I was acutely aware that there was nothing to prevent me from slipping back under the surface. In fact, life could have potentially been worse than before, had Ruth succeeded in taking my home from me.

Fortunately that crisis has been averted as Mr Brooke's gift has allowed me to buy Alan out and secure my home. My only hope is that one day Alan and I will be able to reconcile and reunite as family once more.

If nothing else, these last months have opened a tiny chink in my consciousness and I find myself fantasising about alternative lives for myself – something I would never have dreamed before! I will have to find work soon but haven't quite decided what my direction should be. I don't feel any desire to return to the civil service nor the typewriter, for that matter. Something will present itself, I feel sure.

In the meantime, I have been industrious in my garden. I've put down bulbs for tulips, daffodils, irises and hyacinths. Once so neat and regimented with dull little shrubs, next spring there will be an unruly riot of colour. Over this last week I have spring-cleaned my little house from top to bottom and now this journal will retire to a trunk in the attic.

Everything is ready. Tomorrow I have a train to meet and a new chapter in my life will begin.

Epilogue

2016

The train my mother referred to was bringing my father, William Beaumont, back home. A month later they were married. Iris never returned to the civil service, giving birth to two daughters – my sister, Gwen, and me – in the next three years.

Of course, neither of us were aware of the initial hurdles of our parents' courtship until the discovery of our mother's journal, by which time it was too late to find out more. One can only assume that William 'grasped the nettle', so to speak. We did occasionally see our paternal grandparents but had no contact with our extended family and never had the occasion to meet Sebastian or Topsy. So clearly there was some fall-out there – making William's actions all the more heroic, to my mind.

Growing up in Linnet Lane, we enjoyed simple, uneventful childhoods. It wasn't until we discovered this journal amongst our mother's treasures after her death that we understood the source of her devotion to us as a family. We were a gift she never expected or took for granted.

It's now sixty years since Iris wrote her journal and when I retired from my teaching career last year, I decided to try and track down the people and places she described.

Hammond Brooke is, of course, no longer a figure of mystery, having been the subject of a popular biography. The history of the Rousseau family and the *parfumerie* are also well documented and represented in the famous international perfume museum in Grasse. Also well known is the story of how these two esteemed *parfumeurs*, Monsieur Rousseau and Hammond Brooke, risked everything to smuggle hundreds of refugees – many of them unaccompanied children – out of occupied France.

It appears that during his lifetime, Hammond Brooke was reluctant to reveal the role that he and his colleagues played in saving so many lives. Perhaps simply not in his nature to boast of such things. However, as a result of the publication of his biography their contribution has been recognised by one of the many organisations that assisted in the war effort. Sylvie Moreau, Father Furolo, Didier Lapointe and Dr Renaud have since been awarded for their heroic efforts by the French government, with Monsieur Rousseau and Hammond Brooke receiving posthumous medals of valour.

What led to Vivian Brooke's eventual downfall is not clear. It seems she had been denounced as a Nazi collaborator as early as 1954 but it took three more years for the authorities to process and complete her deportation. I suspect that Hammond initiated this plan to depose her, but less interest in collaborators and France's famously slow bureaucracy meant it took much longer than he hoped.

Already quite notorious in Britain, Vivian had her fair share of adverse publicity as a result of writing her own memoir late in life in which she made it clear she was unrepentant about her fascist leanings. In it, she revealed that prior to taking up residence in Villa Rousseau, she had been forced into exile in Germany to avoid being interned by the British Government as a security risk – as happened to Mr Farley – but no mention, of course, of her involvement with the Gestapo or her wartime activities at Villa Rousseau.

Marcus Geraldson piqued my curiosity, as he did my mother's. Records now released show that he was born in Munich as Gerhard Hass. He was educated in England and his British diction was probably useful in his career as an officer of the German military intelligence, the Abwehr. Most interesting was my discovery that he actually testified against Nazi war criminals at the Nuremberg trials in 1946. In the years after the war these witnesses lived in fear of reprisal and generally changed their identities. Iris noted that Mr Farley was particularly inquisitive about Mr Geraldson, so perhaps he also had his suspicions. It seems doubtful, on the surface of it, that Vivian knew this detail about his background or, if she did, perhaps their allegiance allowed her to overlook this little anomaly.

Many of the other characters Iris met have left little or no trace. Jonathan Fishell-Smith returned to England with Vivian. He assumed his place in the House of Lords for the next few years until he died of alcoholism. Of Alexander and Freddy, nothing is known; nor Mrs Somerville, and Somerville Brassieres went out of business many years ago. Sebastian and Topsy Ballentine were often featured in the society pages; it seems they remained in their marriage and there is no evidence that Sebastian was ever published. Lady Jessica married an American and took up residence there.

Of the Algerian woman, Menna, nothing has been found.

Sylvie Moreau – a close friend of our family – lived the rest of her life at Villa Rousseau with her gifted daughter, Aurélie. She became a grandmother when Aurélie married fellow perfumer, Guillaume Bonfils, and they produced two sons and a daughter.

Parfumerie Rousseau rose from the ashes and once more became a highly respected perfume house. Aurélie, a well-known and glamorous figure, now in her seventies, is still firmly at the helm of the company. The company's signature perfume, *Aurélie*, relaunched in 1982, has become a classic fragrance on par with *Chanel No. 5* and *Joy*. Iris licensed *Iridescence* to the company and that has also become a classic, still popular today.

Finally to Iris and William. Perhaps typical of a couple who met later in life, they were adoring and companionable, the sort who listen to each other intently and are amused by each other's little witticisms. As they grew older, they became increasingly outdoorsy, enjoying long weekend rambles. When William retired they bought a small cottage outside the village of Buttermere in the Lake District, where they spent their days reading and walking the fells. Both my sister and I visited regularly with our own families.

William died early in 1996 and Iris followed that same year. We miss them every day. The cottage was left to my sister and myself. Our children were grown up by then and our first thought was to sell it but somehow we couldn't quite bring ourselves to part with the place where our parents had been so happy.

It was a good decision – both our families come here often to enjoy the wild beauty of Cumbria. Sitting here at my mother's desk, I can look out at the same view of green fells and craggy escarpments that she loved. Iris's journal has been a great gift, and allowed us to get to know our parents in another dimension.

Many people would consider that Iris lived an unremarkable life, which is perhaps fitting. In many ways, she was not remarkable but a sort of everywoman of her time. To my sister and I, her journal speaks volumes of her tolerance, kindness and generous spirit. We see our mother as an ambassador for simple decency. If that's not remarkable – what is?

Kathleen Jackson (née Beaumont)

Acknowledgements

Many thanks to the experts who generously shared their knowledge with me: Benjamin Paul Mabbett (maître de consultation, Roja Dove Haute Parfumerie, Salon de Parfums, Harrods); Ange Skopatie (Salon Manager, Guerlain, Salon de Parfums, Harrods) and Pierre Bonvalot (Sales Assistant, Floris London).

Behind every writer hovers a family of supporters, generous friends who read drafts and offer feedback, expertise and encouragement – and, if we're very lucky, food as well.

A huge thank you to my fabulous friends for all your support: Catherine Hersom-Bowens, Partrick Bowens, Su Mariani, Joseph Furolo, Carolinda Witt, Tracey Trinder, Amanda Woolveridge, Ron Benson, Tula Wynyard, Frances Francis, Christine Winterbotham, Matt and Khim Stone, Jan Reggett, Mark Hampson, Sharon Pittams, Mrs Norah Lowe and Marianne Hurzeler-Schranz.

I continue to be extremely grateful to be published by Penguin Random House, and the enthusiasm and encouragement of Ali Watts, Saskia Adams, Amanda Martin and Louise Ryan is an absolute gift.

Book Club Discussion Notes

1. How would you describe the genre of the book?

2. Could you relate to Iris's loneliness after her father died? Would you have taken the risk she did to do something different?

3. Did you predict any of the twists in the story? What didn't you see coming?

4. What was your favourite moment in the novel?

5. Do you think Farley's death was suicide, misadventure or murder? If murder, who is your chief suspect?

6. What do you think Lady Jessica's motives were?

7. Could Hammond Brooke have changed his situation and been reunited with Sylvie and his daughter?

8. How much did the setting in the South of France and the period contribute to the telling of the story?

9. If you were casting the film, who would you cast as William and Iris?

10. Discuss the importance of the sense of smell. Are there particular smells that trigger memories for you?

11. Do you think the 1950s were a halcyon time? Was life really better/simpler than today?

12. What thematic comparisons, if any, can be drawn between this and the author's first novel, *The Olive Sisters*?

Book Club Discussion Notes

Also by **Amanda Hampson**

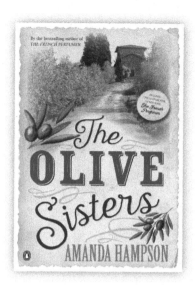

'I open the gate and walk into the field . . . As the sun pours a river of light down this valley, I realise there are hundreds and hundreds of trees and I've seen those silver leaves before, not here in Australia, but shimmering in the groves that grace the terraced hillsides of Tuscany.'

When Adrienne's marketing company goes down, her lifestyle does too. She retreats from the city to the beautiful, abandoned olive grove once owned by her Italian grandparents. A 'tree change' isn't what Adrienne has in mind, however, and life in the country delivers some surprises as she confronts the past and learns the secrets of the Olive Sisters . . .

Old loves, new loves, warm toast and rich traditions are all part of the delicious blend of this absorbing story.

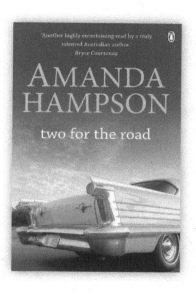

'Another highly entertaining read by a truly
talented Australian author.'
Bryce Courtenay

AMANDA
HAMPSON

two for the road

When Cassie Munro fled her hometown
of Bilkara to follow the charismatic Dan to the
other side of the world, she never expected to return.
Now, devastated by revelations of Dan's betrayal and the
news of a brutal attack on her father, she returns
home with nothing left to lose.

Against her better judgement, she finds herself
battling to save the family business. In the midst of her
struggle, Cassie is reunited with her first love, Mack,
who forces her to confront a guilty secret and the
tragic past they share.

Two for the Road is a powerful and uplifting novel
about one woman's journey of healing, redemption
and letting go of the past.